Know About RSS

Arun Anand

PRABHAT
PRAKASHAN

Published by
PRABHAT PRAKASHAN PVT. LTD.
4/19 Asaf Ali Road,
New Delhi-110 002 (INDIA)
e-mail: prabhatbooks@gmail.com

ISBN 978-93-5322-260-4
KNOW ABOUT RSS
by Shri Arun Anand

Edition
2024

Price
₹ 250.00 (Rupees Two Hundred Fifty only)

Printed at
R-Tech Offset Printers, Delhi

Know About RSS

~~~~~~~~~~~~~~~~~~~~~~~~

For

Seema and Tejas

~~~~~~~~~~~~~~~~~~~~~~~~

"Neither seeks nor avoids, take what comes."

—Swami Vivekananda

Author's Note

FIRST EDITION

There have been a number of books on the Rashtriya Swayamsevak Sangh (RSS). Most of these books have been either anti-RSS or pro-RSS. Interestingly, a significant number of supporters and detractors of the RSS have been carrying on with their arguments without even knowing enough about the RSS itself! This book is an attempt to fill this gap and provide factual information on how the RSS functions and what is its organisational structure. It has taken me around two years to do the research and write this book. So many people helped me with the research that it won't be possible to name all here. I thank everyone of them. I have tried to check and cross check the facts to the best of my ability. I would be glad to know if there are any errors in the book as this would help me to rectify the mistakes and provide a better version in coming editions. I thank all those who have provided support in writing this book, especially the editing and designing team at Prabhat Prakashan.

My friends have been a great source of strength for me. I am blessed to have such friends and a very supportive family. Most of all I thank my readers for taking time out to read this book. I keenly await their feedback.

–Arun Anand

SECOND EDITION

The second edition of this book is an updated version of the first one as I have introduced and additional chapter on the RSS uniform. The monumental decision to replace Khaki shorts which had become symbol of the RSS over last 90 plus years with brown pants made it necessary to write a short chapter on this issue.

I want to thank my readers for their overwhelming response to the first edition of this book. As we go into the second edition, I want to thank all those who gave suggestions to improve it further. My special thanks to Jatin Gandhi for his inputs.

– Arun Anand

Contents

1
The Beginning

The RSS was founded by a medical doctor Dr. Keshav Baliram Hedgewar who devoted much of his life for setting up an organisation which has today grown to become arguably the largest voluntary organisation in the world. RSS has around 50,000 *Shakhas* (a daily gathering of volunteers) around over the country. This does not include millions of volunteers who work in various frontal organisations of RSS. Over a period of time, the RSS and its frontal organisations have come to be known as, *Sangh Parivar* (Sangh family).

Keshav was born on Sunday, 1st April, 1889. He started RSS at the age of around 36 years with a handful of teenagers in Nagpur in 1925. The Hedgewar family originally hailed from Kandkurti village in Telangana. Near the village is the sacred confluence of Godavari, Vanjra and Haridra rivers. This confluence finds mention in several Indian sacred texts. The

place also witnessed a confluence of three robust Indian languages - Kannada, Telugu and Marathi. At one time, the place was a hub of scholars.

But to look out for better opportunities, many Brahmin families left Telangana region. Many of them settled down in Nagpur as the Bhonsle rulers were known to be patrons of Vedic learning. Among them was a Narhari Shastri, whose great grandson was Baliram Pant Hedgewar. In 1853, Nagpur came under the British rule. Vedic learning took a backseat after that as English education took over the former. As a result, many scholars had to resort to priesthood to earn their livelihood. Baliram Pant was one of them. Priesthood didn't bring much money to the family and there were severe financial constraints. Even under such conditions, Baliram along with his wife Revatibai lived a life of contentment. They had in all six children including three sons - Mahadev, Seetaram and Keshav; and three daughters - Saroo, Rajoo and Rangoo. Keshav was the fifth child.

At the age of 13, Keshav lost both his parents to plague. But he continued with his studies amidst quite adverse conditions. He studied in various institutions in Nagpur, Yavatmal and Poona and joined the national movement for freedom. He was greatly influenced by the firebrand nationalism of Lokmanya Tilak. In 1910, he left for Calcutta to study medicine. Trilokynath Chakravarty has written in his book titled 'Thirty Years in Jail', that Keshav Baliram Hedgewar was granted membership of 'Anushilan Samiti', a well-known revolutionary group of freedom fighters at that time. Keshav studied medicine and stayed in Kolkata from 1910 to 1916.

He came back to Nagpur in 1916 and, along with his friend Bhauji Kavre, tried to set up revolutionary groups in Vidharbha and Marathwada regions but these efforts were met with limited success. While trying to set up these groups, he came in contact with the *Akharas* and *Vyayamshalas* (Gymnasiums), in Nagpur. In 1921, there were around 230 *Akharas*. The number increased to 570 by 1931. Dr. Hedgewar had developed a strong network among many of these *Akharas* (which were also local gymnasiums like *Vyayamshalas*, where traditional Indian sports like wrestling, were practised). He developed this network while working for the national freedom movement. In 1921, he participated in the Non-Cooperation Movement and was jailed by the British government on various charges including that of sedition. He read out a written statement in August 1921 while being on trial on the charges of sedition. The written statement said:

1. "It has been charged that my speeches have spread discontent, hatred and feelings of sedition towards the British Empire in the minds of Indians and sown seeds of enmity between Indians and Europeans. And I have been asked to explain. I consider it an affront to the dignity of my great country that a foreign government should subject a native Indian to inquiry and sit in judgement.
2. I do not recognize that there exists in India today any lawfully established government. It will be surprising if anybody should claim so. What obtains today is a regime of usurped authority and a repressive rule deriving power therefrom. The present laws and courts are but handmaids of this

unauthorized regime. In any part of the world, it is only a government of the people constituted for the people that is entitled to administer law. All the other forms of rule are but ruses adopted by deceitful usurpers to loot helpless nations.

3. What I tried to do was to inspire in the hearts of my countrymen an attitude of reverential solicitude for their motherland which at the moment happens to be in a wretched condition. I tried to instill in the people the conviction that India belongs to Indians. If an Indian speaking for his country and spreading the nationalist feeling is regarded as committing sedition, if he cannot speak the truth without promoting hatred between Indians and Europeans, Europeans and those claiming to be the Indian government would do well to bear in mind that the day is not far off when foreigners will be forced to quit this country.
4. The government's version of my speech is neither accurate nor complete. Some stray notes and absurd sentences have been sloppily put together. But that does not bother me. In dealing with Britain and Europeans, I have borne in mind only the basic principles that ought to govern the relationship between two countries. Whatever I have said has been with a view to asserting the birthright of my countrymen and the inevitability of securing our independence. I am prepared to stand by each word that I have uttered. Though I cannot say anything else concerning the charges against me, I am prepared to justify each word and letter of my speech; and I declare that whatever I have said is lawful."

A British judge exclaimed after hearing the statement: "His defense is even more seditious than his original speech!" Dr. Hedgewar was sentenced to one year imprisonment. He was released in July 1922 from Ajani Jail and the same evening a public reception was organised in which the then senior Congress leader Motilal Nehru (father of independent India's first Prime Minister Pandit Jawahar Lal Nehru), and Hakim Ajmal Khan also addressed the gathering. The weekly *Maharashtra* wrote in an article on Dr. Hedgewar's release from jail saying: "No words can adequately describe Dr. Hedgewar's intense spirit of patriotism and selflessness. These traits of his have now become all the more resplendent after the fire ordeal."

There are various accounts as to what propelled Dr. Hedgewar to establish the RSS and devote his complete life for building this organisation. One can say that there was no single incident but several factors which probably motivated him to do so. That included growing

tendency of appeasement of the Muslims which was reflected in some of the moves by Congress such as rejection of a resolution seeking ban on cow-slaughter at the All India Congress Committee Session in 1920.

Along with this, there were certain international developments which were indicating that the Second World War could happen in the years to come. Appaji Joshi who worked closely with Dr. Hedgewar in Congress recounted that he used to predict that Germany would definitely try to take revenge for its defeat in the First World War and that would result in the Second World War. It would take around 20 years and could happen by 1940. Dr. Hedgewar felt that there was a need for a strong cadre-based disciplined organisation which could take advantage of the situation and force the British government to give freedom to India. He strongly felt that the time till 1940 should be used to set up such an organisation and strengthen it so that it could yield a final blow to the British rule.

His experience in the armed revolutionary struggle and the non-violent national struggle under the leadership of Mahatma Gandhi also made him realise that unless a disciplined cadre-based and well-trained nationalistic organisation addresses fundamental issues of building strong nationalistic character, India might not be able to sustain its freedom even if it is able to attain it. The Hindu-Muslim riots following the Non-Cooperation Movement further disillusioned him from the existing tactics deployed by the then leaders of the freedom struggle. He felt that instead of addressing the basic issues, quick fix remedies were prepared which could not provide long-term permanent solutions.

The RSS was founded on the festive day of 'Vijaydashmi', also known as, 'Dussehra', in 1925. This festival marks the victory of good over evil. According to the Indian history, this is the day when Lord Rama, who represented the 'Good', killed King Ravana, a symbol of 'Evil'. It is interesting to note that the RSS was founded with only 15-20 young men and teenagers. Those who were present there included Bhauji Kawre, Anna Sohni, Vishwanathrao Kelkar, Balaji Huddar and Bapurao Bhedi. Initially there were no formal plans. The only agenda was to train the young men making them physically, mentally and intellectually strong to serve the country. The first daily *Shakha* of RSS actually began from May 28, 1926 which had a regular schedule. The place where daily gathering of the initial volunteers/Swayamsevaks of the RSS took place was Mohitewada Ground in Nagpur, which is today a part of the sprawling RSS headquarters complex. Initially, some commands to Swayamsevaks were given in Sanskrit. There were some commands given in English also but they were gradually replaced by the commands in Sanskrit or in local Indian languages over a period of time as the RSS grew. There was a conscious effort to repose and rekindle faith in the Indian culture with Sanskrit as its integral part. Even today, this tradition of giving key commands in Sanskrit continues at thousands of daily *Shakhas*. A Saffron Flag used to be hoisted which is known as *Bhagwa Dhwaj*, in RSS terminology and the first *Shakha* used to begin with a salutation to the Saffron Flag. This tradition continues even today with the beginning and end of every daily *Shakha* happening with a salutation to the Saffron Flag which is designed in such a fashion that it appears to have two flames of fire. The importance, reasoning and philosophy of this particular chore performed at daily *Shakha* has been explained later in this book. The first daily *Shakha* used to end after recitation of a concluding prayer which was a combination of Marathi and Hindi verses. Later on, it was replaced by a Sanskrit prayer. Both these prayers were focussed on nurturing nationalistic feelings

among the Swayamsevaks. The initial prayer for the first *Shakha* could be translated as:

"Salutations to the Motherland
where I am born.
Salutations to the Hindu Land
where I have been brought up.
Salutations to the Land of Dharma
for which may my body fall.
To Her, I salute again and again."

Currently the prayer in Sanskrit is also on similar lines. Its meaning has been explained later in the book along with its importance for the RSS.

It is interesting to note that the RSS got its present name almost six months after it was founded. On April 17, 1926, Dr. Hedgewar called a meeting at his house in which 26 Swayamsevaks participated. A detailed discussion followed to decide the name of the organization for which everyone contributed their ideas. None of them were aware that the name decided at the meeting would one day find huge resonance across the globe in the years to come. Several names were suggested and each of the names was discussed threadbare. Three names were finalised after several rounds of elimination. They were:

1. Rashtriya Swayamsevak Sangh.
2. Jaripataka Mandal.
3. Bhedratoddharak Mandal.

There were more deliberations on these three names and finally the name, 'Rashtriya Swayamsevak Sangh', was chosen.

□

2
The Sangh Parivar

To understand the RSS, one has to understand the broad organisational structure of the Sangh Parivar. Broadly, we can define Sangh Parivar by its composition. It comprises RSS and several frontal organisations. The RSS remains the mentor and provides guidance, direction, support and logistics for the frontal organisations.

Sangh Parivar has a multi-dimensional organisational structure. In the absence of clarity over this aspect, one can get the facts mixed up. Thus, we often see an RSS Prachar Pramukh referred to as *Pracharak Pramukh,* in news reports and panel discussions on television channels. To give you an example, let us take the case of Akhil Bharatiya Vidyarthi Parishad (ABVP), a student organisation that is active in university campuses across the country. It is generally referred to as the student wing of the political outfit Bharatiya Janata Party (BJP). That is not true. On ground, the ABVP and the BJP might be working together closely; many of the BJP's top leaders at present have had their baptism in politics by working initially in the ABVP. They graduated to the BJP later on and are holding crucial posts in the party as well as several important portfolios in the Central and state governments as ministers.

But ABVP has always been and still remains one of the frontal organisations of the RSS. It is not the student wing of the BJP. In fact, the BJP (in its erstwhile form of Bharatiya Jansangh), had set up its student wing under the name of Janta Vidyarthi Morcha in 1978 but it was dissolved in 1980. JVM was founded as in 1978 after ABVP decided to go to villages and work there. As a matter of policy, it decided that it would not contest any student body polls henceforth. So from 1978 to 1980, it was JVM which was contesting student union elections. In 1980, the ABVP changed its stance and decided to start contesting polls again. By that time, the Janata Party had broken and BJP had taken birth. So JVM was effectively disbanded and since then, ABVP is on the forefront of student activities.

Currently, the BJP also supports the ABVP but the latter remains a frontal organisation of the RSS and not that of the BJP.

This confusion has probably also risen as the other major political parties like Congress have student organisations which are directly affiliated to them. But in case of BJP, which itself is an ideological offshoot of the RSS and may be called one of the frontal organisations of the RSS (the BJP-RSS relationship is quite complex and has evolved over a period of time quite differently when we compare it with the RSS' relationship with other frontal organisations comprising Sangh Parivar).

The RSS worked as a single organisation during the first two decades of its existence. There were no frontal organisations. Its focus was to expand and consolidate its base to every nook and corner of the country through the daily gathering of its volunteers ('Swayamsevaks'). This daily gathering is known as *Shakha*. A *Shakha*, still remains the lifeline of *Sangh Parivar*. The next chapter deals in detail about the concept of *Shakha*.

Sangh Parivar can also be loosely translated into, 'The RSS family', which comprises the Rashtriya Swayamsevak Sangh and various frontal organisations which work in diversified constituencies, such as education, urban slums, tribals, labour, farmers, teachers, students, art and culture, etc. Some of the key frontal organisations of the RSS include Rashtriya Sevika Samiti, Vanvasi Kalya Ashram, Sewa Bharati, Akhil Bharatiya Vidyarthi Parishad, Bharatiya Mazdoor Sangh, Bharatiya Kisan Sangh, Vidya

Bharati, Vishwa Hindu Parishad, Pragya Bharati etc. There is virtually no area today ranging from consumer rights to international relations where a frontal organisation of the RSS doesn't work.

The use of 'frontal organisation' in the context of Sangh Parivar has to be looked at not purely in literal terms but in terms of the working relationship between RSS and these organisations. This relationship may be further viewed in the context of the reasoning and rationale behind setting up of these organisations.

Technically, all the frontal organisations of the RSS are autonomous organisations. They have an organisational structure, which is not a replica of the RSS' organisational structure. However, *Pracharaks* (full-time RSS workers) are deputed to work in these organisations by the RSS at different levels.

Despite continuous expansion of the Sangh Parivar, the RSS *Shakha* remains the most important unit of the Sangh Parivar. Why is it so important? How does it operate? What all happens in a *Shakha* and how does it train Swayamsevaks physically, mentally, spiritually and ideologically? We will try to find an answer to these queries in the next chapter. Interestingly, *Shakha* is the smallest and yet the most crucial unit in Sangh Parivar as it still remains the primary, entry point, for getting into the fold of Sangh Parivar. Everyday thousands of new Swayamsevaks join the Sangh Parivar by entering a *Shakha*.

The Swayamsevaks which join these *Shakhas* are often deputed into different frontal organisations of the Sangh Parivar according to their aptitude, skills, inclination and potential after they have spent a few years within the RSS.

Thus, RSS effectively plays an important role in the functioning of all the frontal organisations. The ground rules are clear that the frontal organisations retain their autonomy as far as the day to day functioning is concerned. However, when it comes to crucial policy issues, then the guidance of the RSS is sought. This structure helps the RSS to ensure that all the frontal organisations have synergy at a broad level.

Coming back to the RSS itself, let us have a broad look at its organisational structure.

At the bottom of the organisational pyramid is a *Shakha*. A number of *Shakhas* (could range from 3 to 10) put together are known as *Mandal*. A number of Mandals (generally 5-10), are clubbed together and known as *Nagar*. A number of 'Nagars' form a group called *Zila*.

A number of Zilas put together are known as *Vibhaag*. Five to Fifteen Vibhaags put together are known as *Sambhaag*. A number of Sambhaags put together are known as *Prant*.

For our readers' convenience, I would try to explain this nomenclature. A *mandal* generally comprises a group of colonies or settlements in terms of geographical area. *Nagar* is the Hindi word for 'town'. You may take *Nagar* to be a unit that covers a block or a *tehsil*. A *Zila* generally covers an area equivalent to a district, while a *Sambhaag* would be equivalent to a division. *Prant* translates as 'province'.

A number of *Prants* are clubbed together under the title of *Kshetra* (broadly, it can be translated as a 'region'). Currently, the whole country has been divided into 11 Kshetras by the RSS for its organisational structure.

Each *Kshetra* is headed by a *Kshetra Sanghchalak* and *Kshetra Karyavah.* The latter for all practical purposes is the *defacto* head of each Kshetra. The former is the *dejure* head of the *Kshetra.*

It is important to remember that the organisational structure of the RSS does not adhere to the government's demarcation of the states and districts and towns. For its own organisational purpose, the RSS sometimes divides a larger state into two or more *Prants.*

Contrary to the common perception, the RSS has been quite flexible when it comes to its organisational structure. It has changed several times the areas covered under *Prant* or *Kshetra* or *Mandal* or *Nagar,* to suit the organisational needs. With the emergence of several new states within the country, the RSS too has been making adjustments in its organisational structure to ensure smooth functioning of the organisation.

At present, the whole country has been divided into the following 11 Kshetras (regions):

1. South: It comprises Kerala, South Tamil Nadu and North Tamil Nadu.
2. South-Central: It comprises South Karnataka, West Andhra Pradesh, East Andhra Pradesh (this arrangement was prior to the establishment of Telangana as a separate state out of Andhra Pradesh. It is likely that a re-structuring of this regional grouping under the RSS organisational set-up may happen).
3. West: The Western region has following areas: Konkan, West Maharashtra, Devagiri, Gujarat, Vidarbha.

4. Central: It comprises Malwa, Madhya Bharat, Mahakaushal, Chhattisgarh.
5. North-West: This region has Chittor, Jaipur and Jodhpur.
6. North region: One of the most important regions from RSS' perspective in terms of its strength and impact, it comprises of five *Prants*: Delhi, Haryana, Punjab, Jammu and Kashmir, Himachal Pradesh.
7. West Uttar Pradesh: One should not confuse this with the geographical boundaries of the western part of the Indian state of Uttar Pradesh. From the RSS' perspective, the West Uttar Pradesh is a separate region and it has Uttarakhand, Meerut and Braj.
8. East Uttar Pradesh: This *Kshetra* or region has four Prants: Kanpur, Awadh, Kaashi and Gorakhpur.
9. North-East: This region has North Bihar, South Bihar and Jharkhand.
10. East: It consists of Utkal, South Bengal and North Bengal.
11. Assam: It comprises North Assam, Arunachal Pradesh, South Assam, Manipur.

As mentioned above, there are 11 regions in which RSS has divided its work within the country. Most of the frontal organisations also work within this geographical framework. Each region comprises of a number of *Prants*. Each Prant is headed within the RSS hierarchy by a *Prant Karyavah* and *Prant Sanghchalak*. *Prant Karyavah* is the *de facto* chief of the *Prant* while *Prant Sanghchalak* is the *de jure* chief. The former is generally a relatively young person than the latter one as he is supposed to carry out a vast amount of activities. The *Prant Sanghchalak* is more of a mentor but he is kept in loop in most of the activities and plans.

There are two main bodies of the RSS which take all important decisions, one is known as, *Akhil Bharatiya Karyakarini* (broadly translated as the RSS Central Executive Council), the other body is Akhil Bharatiya Pratinidhi Sabha (ABPS). The latter may be translated in English as 'All India Representative Council'.

The ABPS is considered to be the highest decision-making body of the organisation, which meets annually. The ABPS has representatives from various frontal organisations of the RSS. The RSS functionaries at the *Prant* level and above, take part in the ABPS meetings. The meeting generally lasts for three to four days and is attended by the RSS top brass. A report on the status of the organisation is also presented in this meeting and the challenges faced by the RSS are also discussed. In a way, it is the most crucial event for the RSS as it decides its way forward. The members of the ABPS go back after every meet with a message from the top brass as to what is going to be the broad direction of the RSS work for the coming year. This message is then percolated down to the *Shakha,* level through a series of meetings.

The Akhil Bharatiya Karyakarini comprises the RSS Chief, RSS general secretaries, joint general secretaries, heads and deputy heads of its various wings, such as physical (*Sharirik*), intellectual (*Bauddhik*), Media (*Prachaar*), Public Relations (*Sampark*), Social Services (*Sewa*) and Logistics (*Vyavastha*).

Currently, following officials are the *ex officio* members of the Akhil Bharatiya Karyakarini:

1. *Sarsanghchalak* (The RSS Chief).
2. *Sarkaryavah* (General Secretary).
3. *Sah-Sarkaryavah* (Joint General Secretary): There can be more than one *Sah-Sarkaryavah* in the RSS and generally all are made members of national executive.
4. Akhil Bharatiya Sharirik Pramukh (All India in-charge of physical activities).
5. Akhil Bharatiya Sah-Sharirik Pramukh (All India deputy in-charge of physcial activities).
6. Akhil Bharatiya Bauddhik Pramukh (All India in-charge of intellectual activities).
7. Akhil Bharatiya Sah-Bauddhik Pramukh (All India deputy in-charge of intellectual activities).
8. Akhil Bharatiya Vyavastha Pramukh (All India in-charge of Logistics).
9. Akhil Bharatiya Sah-Vyavastha Pramukh (All India deputy in-charge of Logistics).
10. Akhil Bharatiya Sewa Pramukh (All India in-charge of social services).
11. Akhil Bharatiya Sah-Sewa Pramukh (All India deputy in-charge of social services).
12. Akhil Bharatiya Sampark Pramukh (All India in-charge of public relations).
13. Akhil Bharatiya Sah-Sampark Pramukh (All India deputy in-charge of public relations).
14. Akhil Bharatiya Prachar Pramukh (All India in-charge of media).
15. Akhil Bharatiya Sah-Prachar Pramukh (All India co-incharge of media).

16. Akhil Bharatiya *Pracharak* Pramukh (All India in-charge of RSS workers which work full time): A swayamsevak/volunteer who works full time for the RSS or any of its frontal organisations is called *Pracharak*. We would be discussing role of a *Pracharak* in detail later in this book.
17. Akhil Bharatiya Sah-*Pracharak* Pramukh (All India deputy in-charge of RSS full-time workers).

In March 2014, according to the official records of the RSS, in addition to the above, the All India Executive also had as its members Madandas, Madhubhai Kulkarni, Shankarlal, Mukundrao Panshikar, Sitaram Kedilai, Indresh Kumar, S. Sethumadhvan. The special invitees to this body included N. Krishnappa, Sri Krishna Mothalagh, Sunilpad Goswamy and, Ashok Beri. Generally the, *Kshetriya Pracharak* (each of the 11 regions/kshetra as mentioned above has a senior RSS full-time worker designated as *Kshetriya Pracharak*), are also invited members of the Central Executive Council.

□

3

The RSS 'Shakha'

'Shakha' is a Hindi word. When translated into English, it means 'branch'. The concept of RSS *Shakha* was conceived by its founder Dr. Hedgewar. A *Shakha* is held in an open ground for about an hour. It is held daily round the year without any break. The time of beginning and ending the *Shakha* is to be strictly adhered to and it is not altered. A *Shakha* is held in the morning or evening. Generally, the evening *Shakha* is meant for the students and the younger lot while the morning *Shakha* is meant for the relatively older lot who may not find time in the evening to attend a *Shakha*.

The RSS officially explains the concept of *Shakha* as: "A Saffron Flag (called the *Bhagwa Dhwaj*) flutters in the midst of an open playground. Youths and boys of all ages engage in varieties of indigenous games. Uninhibited joy fills the air. There are exercises, *Suryanamaskar* (a kind of Yoga), sometimes training in skilfully wielding the *Danda* (wooden stick). All activities are totally disciplined. The physical fitness programmes are followed by group singing of patriotic songs. Also forming part of the routine is exposition and discussion of national events and problems. The day's activity culminates in the participants assembling in orderly rows in front of the flag at a single whistle of the group leader, and reverentially reciting the prayer *Namaste Sada Vatsale Matrubhoome* (My salutation to you, loving Motherland). The prayer verses, even as the group leader's various commands, are all in Sanskrit. The prayer concludes with a heart-felt utterance of the inspiring slogan *Bharatmata Ki Jai*. This, in outline, is the *Shakha* of RSS. The participants are the *Sangh Swayamsevaks*."

Underlining the importance of the *Shakha*, the RSS further says, "The *Shakha* is the most effective and time-tested instrument for the moulding of men on patriotic lines - outreaching by far its physical dimension.... The Sangh's method of working is of the simplest kind, and there is hardly anything esoteric about it. Coming together everyday for an hour is the heart of the technique, and

the Sangh has always grown only by personal contact. This is a self-contained mechanism; hence its success.

The daily *Shakha* is undoubtedly the most visible symbol of the Rashtriya Swayamsevak Sangh. The *Shakha* is as simple in its structure as it is grand in conception. No better example can be given to prove the truth of the adage that it takes a genius to simplify a mechanical tool, while even a third-rate engineer can complicate a simple mechanism! After nearly seven decades since the inception of the Sangh, people continue to be surprised as to how such a simple tool as the daily *Shakha* can produce idealists and patriots of such sterling worth, willing to dedicate all their energies and talents to the cause of the Motherland, willing even to shed their lives if need be to protect the honour of the Motherland. Herein lies the extraordinary vision, skill and foresight of Dr. Hedgewar, the Founder of the Sangh."

An RSS *Shakha* begins with the *Swayamsevaks* bowing their head to the flag. This is called *Dhwaj Pranam* (salutation to the flag). The *Dhwaj pranam* is done by putting right hand on center of chest facing towards the ground and bowing your head slightly while standing erect. A *Shakha* ends with a similar *Dhwaj Pranam*. The flag is hoisted everyday and then it is unhoisted at the end of *Shakha,* neatly folded and a Swayamsevak takes it to his home to bring it the next day.

The process of induction into the RSS is informal. Anyone who comes and does *Dhwaj Pranam,* becomes a *Swayamsevak*. There are no forms to be filled, no screening. Each *Shakha* head is known as *Shakha Karyavah*. The second-in-command is designated as *Mukhyashikshak* and the third-in-command is known as *Gan-Shikshak*.

Each *Shakha* is divided into a number of sections for functional purpose. Each section is called *Gatt* and it is headed by one of the experienced Swayamsevaks. The latter is designated as *Gattnayak*.

The emphasis of the RSS ever since its inception has been on running a 'Daily Shakha'. This is a unique feature of the organisation as there is no holiday. The reason cited by RSS functionaries is that in everyday life, we must give atleast one hour for social work. This makes *Shakha*, an inherent part of the Swayamsevaks' daily routine and helps to strengthen the bond with the organisation. Another reason cited is that the volunteers get *Samskars* (good values) by attending *Shakha* and everyday Swayamsevaks in their day-to-day lives get influenced by a number of negative things. So just as a utentsil for eating food or drinking water has to be cleaned everyday to keep oneself healthy, similarly, a human body needs to go through positive physical, mental and spiritual experiences to maintain the level of good values in oneself.

There has been a tradition of naming *Shakha* and each *Shakha* is generally named after one of the great Indians of the past. So, you have *Shakhas*, named after Bhagat Singh, Rajguru, Sukhdev, Abhimanyu, Arjun, etc.

For several decades, the emphasis of the RSS was primarily on 'Daily Shakhas'. However, as many RSS Swayamsevaks went to different countries and settled there, they started holding weekly *Shakha*.

An interesting offshoot of this flexibility imbibed by the RSS is, "IT (Information Technology) *Shakha*." This is a virtual *Shakha* meant primarily to allow, "periodic connect" with the IT professionals. IT *Shakhas* are mostly weekly in nature and there are one or two coordinators, who generally hold it online. The, 'IT *Shakhas*', have been growing robustly ever since their inception.

So, the RSS has daily *Shakha*, weekly *Shakha* as well as the IT *Shakha*. The daily *Shakha* is also of two types, morning *Shakha* and evening *Shakha*. The morning *Shakha* is generally attended by the adults and the older lot. The evening *Shakhas* focus at the students.

On the basis of the age group, RSS has categorised all *Swayamsevaks*, who attend any kind of *Shakha* into four categories, "*Shishu* (kid), *Baal* (Child), *Tarun* (adolescent), *Praud* (old)." The broad age criteria for these categories are five years and below, 6-12 years, 13-18 years, above 50 years.

The philosophy guiding the concept of an RSS *Shakha* has been elaborated upon in, "The Story of the Sangh" (written by someone from the RSS under the interesting pseudonym of 'A Swayamsevak"). It says, during and after the *Shakha* timings, Swayamsevaks interact in an extremely friendly and homely atmosphere. The members of the *Shakha* also maintain a warm and cordial relationship with the members of the Swayamsevaks' families, be they young or old, men or women. As a result, new persons who come to participate in the *Shakhas* feel delighted and at home and unlike others in the society, the Swayamsevak never feels that social work is burden to him. Slowly, but steadily, seeing the dedication of senior *Shakha* workers, the Swayamsevaks start giving more and more time for the *Shakhas*. Simultaneously, in keeping with each one's ability, they are given some small responsibilities. They are also provided with adequate training to effectively carry out these responsibilities. In the process, a succession of trainees grow to become

trainers and the continuity from one generation to another is maintained. It is through this process that some of the more capable from among those who are trained thus choose to dedicate their full-time for the Sangh. They are sent to various parts of the country depending on where there is necessity. Such workers who are assigned full-time work are known as *Pracharaks*.

The 'Daily Shakha' of RSS has a permanent schedule with time fixed for every activity. The focus is on all three aspects, physical fitness, mental strength and spirituality. Here is a break-up of the daily schedule of a *Shakha*:

- ***Beginning of the Shakha followed by warm-up through jogging/running (5 minutes)***
- ***Yoga, Suryanamaskar and games (40 minutes)***
- ***Recital of Sanskrit Shlokas known as Subhashit/ Amrit Vachan or patriotic songs. There are thousands of songs written by the RSS functionaries themselves, which are quite popular within the RSS. Every week four-five days the poems, songs and Sanskrit hymns are recited, there are some discourses related to the contemporary issues or ideological aspects at least twice or thrice***

a week. These activities are interchangeable and a Shakha Karyavah (who heads the Shakha), has the flexibility to chose which of the activities should be taken up on particular days of the week. (10 minutes)

- ***Prayer and end of Shakha for the day. (5 minutes)***

That comes precisely to be one hour or 60 minutes. The unique thing about a daily *Shakha* is that the timings are adhered to with precision, especially when it comes to the beginning or end of the *Shakha*. One may say that it is done with military precision. The discipline to follow the time schedule strictly is visible in every activity of the RSS and its affiliated organisation and the only reason is the importance of, 'time schedule', imbibed in Swayamsevaks through their daily visits to *Shakha*.

An important aspect of daily *Shakha* is the 'Games' which they play. The aim of these games is to inculcate a spirit of nationalism. *Kabaddi* and *Kho-Kho*, the two traditional Indian contact sports are played regularly at *Shakha*. Whenever there is a get-together of various *Shakhas*, the spirit of competitiveness is quite high in these matches. There are no 'prizes' for the winners. The game is played for the love of the sport. Even as for decades, Indian sports like *Kabaddi* and *Kho-Kho* were losing their sheen at the official sports platforms within the country, these two sports were being kept alive by the RSS as thousands of children and young men played it every morning or evening at the RSS *Shakhas* across the country and sometimes offshore also where many RSS *Shakhas* are held.

Let us have a look at some of the popular games played at the RSS *Shakhas*:

1. **Mai Shivaji (I am Shivaji):** The game is an outdoor one. Any number of players can play it. One person is designated as 'Shivaji' (the name has been taken from famous Maratha King Chhattrapati Shivaji whose exploits against Mughals are idealised by the RSS. He is one of the most revered personalities for Swayamsevaks for his bravery, staunch commitment to Hinduism and benevolence as a King). The game starts with one Swayamsevak running after the Swayamsevak designated as 'Shivaji' to touch his body. During the chase any Swayamsevak can cut this run through the gap between the former two and while doing that, he has to say loudly *Mai Shivaji* (I am Shivaji). So, now the Swayamsevak chasing the earlier 'Shivaji', has to run after the new one. The objective of this game is that a Swayamsevak should try to protect someone like Shivaji and take the attack on himself and the second one is that every Swayamsevak should feel like 'Shivaji' and imbibe the qualities of the Maratha King.
2. **Mitra-Raksha (Defending a Friend):** The Swayamsevaks will stand in a circle and form a human chain by holding hands. There will be one person inside who is the 'friend', there is one person outside the circle who is an 'enemy'. The 'enemy' has to break into the circle and touch the 'friend'. Everyone else has to ensure not to allow the 'enemy' to come close to the friend. The 'friend' can move inside or outside at his will, while the 'enemy' can also move inside or outside the circle

but if he is inside, then he would be stopped from going outside by the rest. If the 'enemy' is outside the circle, then he would be stopped from coming inside. While saving the 'friend', the circle formed by joining hands shouldn't break. The apparent aim of this particular game is to inculcate the sense of 'protecting friends'. This strengthens the bond of friendship among Swayamsevaks.

3. **Dilli Hamari (Delhi is Ours):** In a small circle where the boundaries are clearly marked, one Swayamsevak will stand in the middle and shout *Dilli kiski* (Delhi belongs to whom), rest of the Swayamsevaks will answer by shouting, *Dilli Hamari* (Delhi is ours). This call will be repeated three times and then every Swayamsevak will try to enter the circle by pushing the others out. At the end of the game, whoever is standing in the circle is the winner. The same game has another version also where, 'Delhi', is replaced by Kashmir or, at times, 'Lahore' also. This game is apparently aimed at inculcating the sense of patriotism by making Swayamsevaks realise that the capital of

the country, which is Delhi or New Delhi, belongs to each one of them. Similar is the case of 'Kashmir'. When Swayamsevaks give a call for 'Lahore is Ours', that reflects the long-standing dream of RSS to have an, *Akhand Bharat* (an integrated India, which was divided into India and Pakistan in 1947).

There are around 50 such games listed in, '*Shakha* Surabhi', one of the important publications of RSS, which is a primer for the Swayamsevaks and various functionaries, as far as conducting daily activities at *Shakha* is concerned.

These games are played under the supervision of *Ganashikshak*, and all the functionaries play these games on equal footing. The word *Ganashikshak*, comprises two words *Gana*, which broadly means a group of persons and *Shikshak*, which is a Hindi word for 'instructor'. Each daily *Shakha* has generally one *Ganashikshak*. In his absence, the other senior functionaries often take the charge and perform his duty. The average number of Swayamsevaks attending a daily *Shakha* range from broadly 10 to 50.

The instructions while playing the games are given in 'Sanskrit' and the instructor also uses a whistle. The senior functionaries also use a whistle to perform most important activities in a daily *Shakha*. The RSS leadership over the years has been able to do extensive detailing which is available in its manuals in terms of how to conduct the daily activities at *Shakha*.

Indian martial arts termed as *Niyudh* and the traditional art of fighting with a wooden stick known as *Dand yudh*, are also taught at the *Shakha*. However, the time devoted to them is not much and it is part of the daily schedule of the *Shakha*.

An RSS *Shakha* begins daily with a ceremonial hoisting of the Saffron Flag and ends with the lowering down of the flag in a prescribed manner. While these two ceremonies happen, all Swayamsevaks stand in columns in straight lines. They bow their head to the flag on the command of the, *Mukhyashikshak,* at the beginning and end of the *Shakha* after which the flag is lowered down. A particular Swayamsevak is entrusted to take back the flag to his home. The Saffron Flag is known as *Bhagwa Dhwaj* (Bhagwa stands for Saffron while Dhwaj is the Sanskrit word for a flag). The Saffron Flag is hoisted and lowered at all the outdoor and most of the indoor functions of the RSS. It is the most revered element for any Swayamsevak.

□

4
The Saffron Flag

The Saffron Flag, commonly known as, *Bhagwa Dhwaj*, is considered to be the *Guru* (the Master) by all Swayamsevaks. When the RSS was started, several Swayamsevaks wanted its founder Dr. Hedgewar to be designated as the *Guru*, as he was the most revered figure amongst them and every Swayamsevak looked upto him as an ideal. But Dr. Hedgewar decided that the Saffron Flag should be the *Guru*. Every year on the day of *Vyas Poornima*, according to the Indian calendar, the Saffron Flag is worshipped formally. This is known as *Gurupuja* and is one of the six main festivals which the RSS celebrates every year.

The first *Gurupuja* in RSS was organised in 1928 where the *Bhagwa Dhwaj*, was formally worshipped as the *Guru* for the first time. Since then, there has been no break in this tradition and the Saffron Flag continues to occupy the highest pedestal in the RSS hierarchy. It is the 'Supreme', even above the *Sarsanghchalak* (RSS Chief).

Why is Saffron Flag treated as the Master or the Supreme by the RSS? The question has baffled many as there has been a general tradition even in India that many

spiritual and religious institutions and organisations have had their founders as the *Guru* and they are worshipped by the followers. In the rich Indian tradition of, *Bhakti movement* and even in the contemporary era, there is no dearth of individuals treated as the *Guru*. In fact, the decision to have the saffron Flag as the *Guru* is a unique move even if one goes into the recent world history. A Saffron Flag being the ultimate Master in a mammoth organisation that could be called one of the largest voluntary organisations of the world is worth pondering upon. Many in the RSS have tried to explain this interesting aspect of the organisation.

According to RSS ideologue H.V. Seshadri, *Bhagwa Dhwaj,* has been a venerated symbol of the national culture and tradition of Bharat (ancient name of India) since ages. When Hedgewar started the Sangh, he placed the Bhagwa before all Swayamsevaks as the supreme symbol of all national ideals. He eulogised it as the *Guru* and established the tradition of Gurupooja on the Vyaspoornima day. That is the day when Swayamsevaks place their devotional offerings at its *altar* (this is known as *Guru Dakhsina*). The Bhagwa-coloured flags have since been adopted by several mass organisations like BMS (Bharatiya Mazdoor Sangh) ABVP (Akhil Bharatiya Vidyarathi Parishad), VKA (Vanvasi Kalyan Ashram), BKS (Bharatiya Kisan Sangh) and Vishwa Hindu Parishad (VHP). The daily fluttering of Bhagwa in tens of thousands of places all over the country in *Shakhas*, with its mass display on occasions by these other organisations, has carved for the Bhagwa a unique place as the national symbol *par excellence* in the hearts of the people."

Interestingly, Seshadri also explains the struggle associated with the acceptance of the Saffron Flag outside the RSS. He says, "It was in the field of labour that the toughest challenge was posed to the acceptance of Bhagwa; for, the trade union field the world over has for long been dominated by the Red flags. But the BMS took up the Bhagwa and forcefully presented it as the traditional national symbol representing universal welfare. The Saffron has now become popular and adorns all BMS programmes. When a huge BMS procession waded its way through the streets of Calcutta, a left-dominated metropolis, during the 6th BMS National Conference in March 1981, citizens were surprised to see the Saffron Flags instead of the usual red in the hands of thousands of workers. Prominent newspapers of Calcutta also commented on this as an altogether new phenomenon."

N.H. Palkar, Karyavah (Chief) of the RSS in Maharashtra Province wrote an interesting book exclusively on the Saffron Flag of the RSS. The book was originally written in Marathi and got published in 1958. A Hindi translation of the same was later reproduced. This 76-page book examines the origin of the Saffron Flag and dates it back to Vedic period.

Palkar says, "The Saffron Flag has always been respected in the Hindu social life...it finds mention in Vedic literature as 'Arunketu'."

He further adds that the Saffron Flag has been a source of inspiration to get up and fight back for the Hindus whenever they faced attacks by the foreigners. The Saffron Flag was used as a well-planned measure to motivate Hindus to fight back and protect the nation.

Palkar explains several historical incidents to establish the national character of the Saffron Flag. Some of them are being given here.

"*Guru* Gobind Singh (the Sikh *Guru*), who led thousands of Sikh warriors to protect the Hindus, also wielded a Saffron Flag. The Saffron Flag is a symbol of revival of Hinduism and the followers of *Guru* Gobind Singh won Kabul and Kandhar in Afghanistan under the leadership of Sikh General Hari Singh Nalwa during Maharaja Ranjit Singh's time," says Palkar.

He goes on to add, "Just like Punjab when Muslims attacked Rajasthan, the Rajput warriors under the leadership of Rana Sanga and Maharana Pratap fought back under the Saffron Flag. Chhatrapati Shivaji and his followers fought the battle of freedom under the Saffron Flag to establish the Hindu Kingdom."

Palkar elaborates by citing historical example from the history of South India when the Kings of Vijaynagar Kingdom were engaged in fierce battles to push back the attacks from Muslims. The conclusion is clear that Saffron is the colour of valour and sacrifice for nation.

Palkar also explains the importance of the Saffron colour in the famous spiritual tradition of India commonly known as *Bhakti movement*, which is credited with the revival of a reformed Hinduism in the medieval era.

"The Saffron Flags flutter on the top of innumerable temples and (Hindu) monasteries of India," says Palkar pointing out that along with valour, the Saffron Flag is also associated with the ideals of renunciation.

Palkar mentions that it was Saffron Flag around which the revolutionaries rallied during first war of India's independence from the British Rule in 1857. In the epilogue of his book, he concludes, "After going through the complete history of *Bhagwa Dwaj*, one realises that it is not possible to separate the Hindu society from this flag. Bhagwa Dhwaj is the natural symbol of Hindu society, i.e. Hindu Rashtra (country)."

What Palkar has written in this section of the book forms one of the fundamental rationales that RSS Swayamsevaks are often explained in the intellectual discourses in the RSS *Shakhas* and training camps when it comes to a discussion on the importance of *Bhagwa Dhwaj*.

Palkar succinctly puts it, "Hindu nation, Hindu society, Hindu religion, Hindu culture, Hindu way of life and Hindu philosophy are all integrally related to the Saffron Flag. The Saffron Flag is capable of inspiring qualities like renunciation, sacrifice, valour, patriotism, etc."

"The Saffron Flag is a witness to the constant struggle and victories of the Hindu society.... One can't imagine Hindu *dharma* (the word 'religion' is not used here as according to many scholars Hinduism is a *dharma*, i.e. way of life and it can't be equated to a religion which is related to, certain set of rituals), Hindu culture and Hindu nation without the Saffron Flag. Culture is the lifeline of any country. Hindu culture is the lifeline of our country and the Saffron Flag is a symbol of Hindu culture."

Palkar makes a very significant statement when he says, "The existence of the Saffron Flag doesn't depend on the fact whether it has been granted any official (probably he wanted to convey recognition by government authorities) status or not. That is why even today, the Saffron Flag is worth worshipping for political parties, social outfits, sects or sub-sects.

The Saffron Flag is a symbol of aspirations of the Hindu society and it has that energy to provide inspiration to realise these aspirations. This energy may not be embodied but it does get revealed in the form of a united Hindu society."

The most important tenet which guides the RSS philosophy regarding treating Bhagwa Dhwaj or the Saffron Flag as its *Guru* is that an individual can fall from grace or may have some weaknesses but the Saffron Flag can't.

It is apparent that the decision to choose Saffron Flag as the *Guru* in RSS was taken primarily due to three reasons:

First, to make an organisation stand unitedly and grow, a flag remains historically one of the most potent means.

Second, the cultural nationalism which is one of the key building blocks of the RSS' ideology finds its most comprehensive reflection in the Saffron Flag.

Third, the RSS wanted to ensure that it does not become a person-centric organisation by putting a symbol of cultural nationalism at the highest pedestal instead of an individual. This seems to have worked well for the organisation which has witnessed a massive expansion of its base in all walks of life over more than nine decades without getting mired into a controversy over the issue of 'Head' of the organisation. It is astounding not to have a war of succession in any such organisation. The credit, to a large extent, should also go to such decisions of granting supreme status to the Saffron Flag.

Thus, everyone in the Sangh Parivar bows their head in front of the Saffron Flag with great reverence, including the *Sarsanghchalak,* i.e. the RSS Chief. And at the RSS *Shakhas,* these fluttering flags convey the spirit of cultural nationalism everyday, round the year. This could, perhaps, explain how the RSS Swayamsevaks find themselves so closely connected with the idea of cultural nationalism.

Guru Dakshina

Every RSS *Shakha* organises, *Guru Dakshina,* a programme for its Swayamsevaks on a particular day in the year. There are primarily two reasons for organising this programme. First, to carry forward the age-old revered tradition of *Guru-Shishya* (Master-Disciple) tradition of ancient India. The students used to stay in the Ashrams of saints in ancient India and on completion of their education and training, used to offer *Dakshina,* as a mark of respect for the Master. In the Hindu tradition, the value of the 'offering' did not matter, what really mattered was the sense of gratitude with which the *Dakshina,* was given. The teachers used to accept whatever was offered with an equal sense of contentment.

This sacred tradition was revived by the RSS in modern times in its *Shakha,* right since its inception and is performed till date. It is a simple ceremony which is held indoor. Generally, it is held in a hall where around 50-

100 people can sit. The ceremony is generally held in the morning. The dress code is, 'all white'. On the day of Guru Dakshina, the Swayamsevaks prefer to wear the traditional Indian dress of *Kurta-Payjama* or *Kurta-Dhoti*.

The Saffron Flag is hoisted within the big room/hall auditorium and a ceremonial Indian earthen lamp is lighted. The framed photographs of the RSS founder Dr. Hedgewar and the second RSS Chief, MS Golwalkar (fondly addressed as *Guruji* within the RSS) are placed alongside. Incensed sticks are also placed.

All the Swayamsevaks sit on the floor where a number of *daris* (a kind of Indian carpet made of thick cloth used at homes generally), or clothe sheets are laid. Before that the room is properly cleaned. There is pin-drop silence and it is mandatory for Swayamsevaks to reach well in time before the scheduled beginning of the programme. All of them sit in rows. Prior to the beginning of the programme, they are given a plain white envelope with their names written on it by the *Shakha* head, i.e. Mukhyashikshak/*Shakha* Karyavah. These envelopes are often delivered to them personally at their homes along with the information regarding schedule f the *Guru-Dakshina*.

The attempt is to inform all the Swayamsevaks who has ever attended a *Shakha* in that area even once. This is probably an effective way to keep the new recruits connected to the RSS even if they are not attending the *Shakha*.

The programme of *Guru Dakshina* is simple but very impressionable atleast for the newcomers due to the prevailing spiritual atmosphere. Anyone who has ever attended *Guru Dakshina*, with an open mind would vouch for it that the atmosphere is unique and leaves a long-lasting impression, especially on the younger minds.

The Indian incense sticks are lighted, there is an aroma of sobriety all around. A few Sanskrit shlokas are recited by everyone praising the *Guru* and expressing their gratitude. The Swayamsevaks also sing together some patriotic songs remembering the 'golden age' of India and vowing to bring back that age by being part of the nation-building process. Then Swayamsevaks get up one by one, offer some flower petals kept in a tray near the Saffron Flag, bow their head to the flag with their straight right palm horizontally parallel to the ground (this is the way RSS Swayamsevaks always bow their heads in front of the Saffron Flag during all programmes including daily *Shakha*). This is called *Dhwaj Pranam,* by the RSS, i.e. greeting the Saffron Flag with respect. The Swayamsevaks then place the envelopes which have some money in it (there is no fixed amount which one has to keep in the envelope and no one asks about it). The envelope is closed, so no one knows who has put in how much money. The Swayamsevak again does *Dhwaj Pranam* and comes back and sits at his place in the row and the next Swayamsevak then goes and performs *Guru Dakshina,* in a similar way.

After *Guru Dakshina,* there is a brief intellectual discourse delivered by either one of the senior RSS functionaries invited for the same or by any other guest who has been invited for the special occasion. The RSS encourages its *Shakha* Chiefs to utilise the '*Guru Dakshina*', programme to invite the local professors, doctors, retired members of the armed forces or any other well-known person as the 'main speaker', for the programme. This helps to expand the organisation its outreach by getting non-RSS members involved. The general experience has been that anyone who is not an RSS Swayamsevak and comes to the programme of *Guru Dakshina* for the first time as a main speaker goes back with such a strong impression that he remains a lifelong supporter and friend of the RSS.

At the end of the programme, there is the usual RSS Prayer and then everyone disburses.

Here a few things must be mentioned regarding the concept of *Guru Dakshina*.

Guru Dakshina was conceived in the earlier days as a two-pronged measure to collect funds from within the organisation to support its expansion and to establish the importance of Saffron Flag as the "Supreme Master."

With the passage of time, the programme of *Guru Dakshina,* became a great medium to connect with even those Swayamsevaks who generally may not attend the RSS activities regularly. At least once in a year, the RSS is able to connect with them.

Over the years, as the RSS expanded with its frontal organisations working in several spheres of society and its Swayamsevaks being spread out all over the country, there are specific *Guru Dakshina,* programmes held in the RSS Offices or at other places for those who may not be attending the RSS *Shakha* but would be working in some other organisations. So you have special *Guru Dakshina* programmes for journalists, bureaucrats, senior RSS functionaries, members of RSS frontal organisations.

The most important lesson that can be drawn from the *Guru Dakshina,* programme is the honesty with which all the money is handled and how money is not used as the criteria for judging a Swayamsevak's place in the organisation.

After every *Guru Dakshina* programme, the money is counted by the Chief Organiser (Mukhyashikshak/*Shakha* Karyavah), a list is prepared in which names of persons and the money kept in their envelopes is recorded in writing and handed over to the designated senior functionary who further hands it over to the seniors and then at the Central level, all the money is utilised for supporting the RSS activities. No one keeps a single *paisa* and there has never been a case of any 'corruption', in the whole history of RSS. The RSS functionaries attribute all this to the 'character-building', carried out at the RSS *Shakhas* day in and day out. Even some critics of the RSS would agree that in a corruption-ridden society, this is a successful model which can be followed. In fact, the key for all the successful RSS activities is 'Strong Character', according to the RSS functionaries.

The *Guru Dakshina* is performed once a year. Generally a fortnight or a month's deadline is fixed within which all RSS *Shakhas* and other affiliated organisations have to organise, '*Guru Dakshina*'. It is a tradition which has never been broken in the RSS and is considered to be the most revered and sacred one.

□

5
The Festivals

The RSS celebrates six festivals at different times of the year:

1. Vijaydashmi Mahotsav
2. Makar Sankranti Mahotsav
3. Varsh Pratipada Mahotsav
4. Hindu Samrajya Dinotsav
5. Gurupurnima Mahotsav
6. Rakshabandhan Mahotsav

Why did the RSS choose these six festivals? The philosophy behind this move has been explained in a publication titled. *Sangh Utsav*. The comments in *Sangh Utsav*, are based on the views expressed by MS Golwalkar, the second RSS chief and Bala Saheb Deoras, the third RSS Chief.

"The RSS has chosen these festivals as they synergise with its objectives and name. One must understand here that Sangh has not created any new festival. But these festivals are of national importance and the Hindu society has been celebrating them since times immemorial."

There is one exception to this: 'Hindu Samrajya Dinotsav', which was not celebrated at national level till the RSS included it in its list. And *Sangh Utsav*, accepting this fact, adds, " Hindu Samrajya Dinotsav is a festival that inspires an awakening in the society. That is why Sangh has included it in the list of other traditional festivals."

The reason for celebrating these festivals is further explained, "Memories of the great personalities who made sacrifices are associated with these festivals. So we (the RSS Swayamsevaks), awaken the society through these festivals."

More importantly the celebrations of these festivals help the RSS to expand its base. The festivals are generally celebrated at the *Shakha* level. "Once a *Shakha* decides to celebrate the festival, this helps to showcase the RSS' ideology and work, to the local community. It helps to bring the local community closer to the Sangh. Thus, these festivals play an important role in creating a conducive environment for the expansion of the RSS."

1. **Vijaydashmi Mahotsav:** Though all festivals are of equal importance for the Swayamsevaks but this one holds a special place in their heart as the RSS was founded on *Vijaydashmi* (September 27, 1925). Every year Vijaydashmi falls on a different day according to the Hindu calendar. The festival of Vijaydashmi is celebrated almost in every part of the country and there are several tales, legends associated with it, the most popular being the defeat of the demon king 'Ravana', by Lord Rama, one of the most revered God figures in India. According to the Hindu epic 'Mahabharata', the Pandavas' 14-year exile had come to an end this day and they had worshipped their 'weapons'. In

the Hindi heartland, this ceremony is also called *Shastra-Pujan*. The RSS Swayamsevaks perform this symbolic ceremony of *Shastra-Pujan*, on this day. This is to inculcate the qualities of bravery and valour among the Swayamsevaks. The festival is associated with the rich cultural history of India and there are several ancient tales, anecdotes and legends associated with it. All of them have, however, one common message: "The victory of good over the evil." There has been a tradition in the RSS that the *Sarsanghchalak* of the day delivers a public speech at Nagpur on this day in a function where thousands of RSS Swayamsevaks are present.

2. **Makar Sankranti Mahotsav:** It is also known as Makar Sankranti. It is one of the most important festivals of Hindus and is celebrated in the month of 'Magh' (January). The ascent of the Sun begins to the north on this day. This movement is known as *Uttarayan* also. The festival marks the commencement of the sun's journey to the Northern Hemisphere (Makara raashi). The RSS celebrates this as a festival for several reasons. This

is the time period which signifies journey from darkness to light, from falsehood to truth and from death to elixir of life. Indians take holy dip in the rivers on this sacred day. Historically, this festival is associated with several important events. After the daily RSS *Shakha*, a mix of sesame seed (*Til*) and Jaggery (*Gur*) is distributed among the Swayamsevaks. Senior RSS functionaries deliver lectures about the importance of this age-old festival for the society at the RSS *Shakhas*. At times, several *Shakhas* get-together and celebrate it jointly also. "This is the time when Swayamsevaks have to think what they have done individually for the country. A new beginning has to be made on this occasion and ...Swayamsevaks should take a resolve that they will work selflessly for the welfare of the society," says RSS publication *Sangh Utsav*, while explaining the importance of this festival for the organisation.

3. **Varsh Pratipada Mahotsav:** The RSS celebrates it as the 'Hindu New Year'. According to the traditional Indian knowledge and scriptures, Lord Brahma had begun creating the universe on this particular day. There are several important events associated with this day. Emperor Vikramaditya had defeated the Shaka invaders and forced them to flee from India. So a new Hindu calendar had begun on this day called *Vikrami Samvat*. This remains one of the most popular calendars in several parts of the country, especially in the rural India. Lord Rama's coronation as the King of Ayodhya happened on this day. One of the greatest

Indian reformers of modern era, Maharishi Dayanand had set up *Arya Samaj*, on this day. India's official national calendar, Shak Samvat, also begins on the same day. Incidentally, the Founder of the RSS, Dr. Hedgewar was also born on the same day. According to Sangh Utsav, "This festival marks the end of an old year and the beginning of the new year. So it is time to review the work of the past year and plan for the upcoming year." The Swayamsevaks wear full RSS uniform on this day at *Shakha* and before the Saffron Flag is hoisted, a special salute is given in the memory of the founder of RSS. This salute is called, *Aadya Sarsanghchalak Pranam*. The RSS band known as *Ghosh* plays wherever possible. Several RSS *Shakhas* often get together on this occasion and competitions are held. Key RSS functionaries deliver intellectual discourse on this day. At times, a leading figure from society is also called as the chief guest.

4. **Hindu Samrajya Diwas:** This festival is different from the rest of the festivals celebrated by the RSS. "While the rest of the festivals celebrated by the RSS are also celebrated by the common people outside RSS also, it is the only festival which is generally not celebrated in the society at mass level. In fact, many people even don't know that a historical event took place, which deserves to be celebrated." (Sangh Utsav). The festival is celebrated to commemorate the coronation of Maratha warrior and King Chhatrapati Shivaji. The coronation was done on May 19, 1674. Along with this coronation, a Hindu empire came into

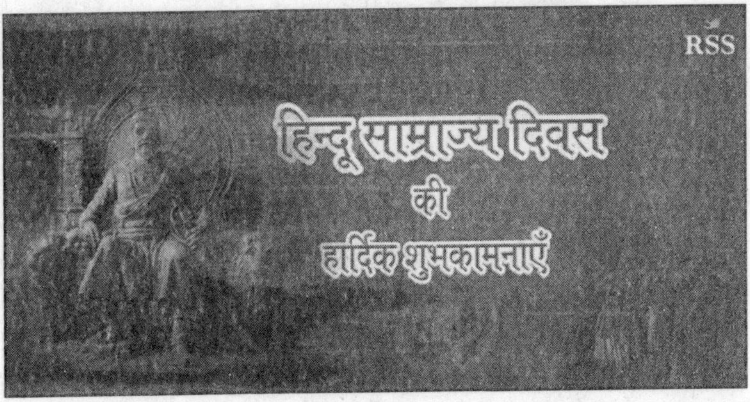

existence officially as Shivaji himself announced that day, "Hindu self rule should be established, that is the will of the God." He also said, "This kingdom does not belong to Shivaji but to the *dharma*."

"The Hindus were at the receiving end when this momentous event happened and it electrified the Hindu consciousness across the country. "It was the time when Hindus could not even think of being rulers. The moral of Hindus was so low that they couldn't think of reaching up to that level and they had accepted that only Muslims can become rulers and Hindus can only serve them. In such a desperate situation, Shivaji's act of setting up a Hindu empire boosted the moral of the Hindus immensely. So, if we have to move on our path rightly, it is imminent to remember great men like Shivaji who created history." The festival is celebrated at the RSS *Shakha* by worshipping portraits of Shivaji and his master (*Guru*) Samarth Ramdas. The famous letter written by Shivaji to Rajput King Jai Singh is also read on this occasion,

The letter calls upon the Rajput warrior not to shed the blood of Hindus for Mughals and exhorts him to join Shivaji for the greater cause. On this occasion anecdotal tales of Shivaji's valour are shared by the senior Sangh functionaries in the form of intellectual discourses with Swayamsevaks. At times, several *Shakhas* get-together to celebrate this festival. Tributes are offered to Shivaji and Samartha *Guru* Ramdas. The role played by Shivaji's mother Jijabai and his other colleagues like Taana Ji is also dwelt upon in great detail. Jijabai, along with Shivaji, remains one of the most revered figures in Sangh Parivar for the way she motivated her son to fight back the Mughals and set up *Dharma Rajya*, which may be broadly translated as the 'Rule of the righteousness." As part of the celebrations, Swayamsevaks also recite patriotic songs especially penned for the festival by many writers and published by the RSS publications.

5. **Gurupurnima Mahotsav:** In Hinduism, the place of the Master (*Guru*) is considered to be even above the God. This festival is an occasion to express gratitude to the Master for showing the right way to live the life and imparting knowledge. In the RSS, as mentioned earlier in the book, the *Bhagwa Dhwaj* (Saffron Flag) is the *Guru*. So the Swayamsevaks worship the *Bhagwa Dhwaj*, on this day. The festival is celebrated in the Hindu month of Aashaad and on a full-moon day. The day is also known as *Aashaadi Poornima*. The Swayamsevaks generally wear white clothes

(preferably traditional Indian dresses like *dhoti-kurta* or *kurta-payjama*), and the black RSS cap on this occasion and worship the Saffron Flag by offering floral tributes. It is followed by intellectual discourses on the importance of the Guru in life and Swayamsevaks are reminded why RSS chose Saffron Flag instead of an individual as the *Guru*. The message conveyed through this festival is subtle but quite meaningful that the ideology is bigger than any individual and the RSS is not an individual-centric organisation but an ideology-driven outfit.

6. **Rakshabandhan:** This is a very popular festival in India and celebrated by almost all the communities and religions. The sisters tie a thread commonly known as *Rakhi*, to their brother's wrist as a mark of the commitment of the latter to protect them. There are several historical incidents and tales associated with it. The RSS Swayamsevaks celebrate Rakashabandhan by tying threads to each others' wrists as a symbol of their commitment to protect each other and stand by each other, whatever the circumstances may be. This helps to strengthen a feeling of brotherhood among Swayamsevaks. The RSS celebrates this day as *Adhiktam Sankhya Diwas* (Maximum Attendance Day). The Swayamsevaks at every *Shakha* try to have the maximum number of persons attending *Shakha* that day. The attempt is, get all those who have ever attended the *Shakha* atleast once and to get many new Swayamsevaks also who attend the *Shakha* for the first time on this particular day. This

helps to consolidate as well as expand the reach of the RSS *Shakhas*.

The public parks where *Shakhas* are held wear a real colourful look this particular day as the attendance on many *Shakhas* cross more than 100. With so many persons playing various games simultaneously, singing patriotic songs and raising slogans like, *Bharat Mata ki Jai* (Long Live Mother India), one often sees hundreds of bystanders watching this impressive show even as the Swayamsevaks continue with their disciplined activities unperturbed by all the attention they attract. After the *Shakha* starts, the sacred thread is tied to the Saffron Flag first and the Swayamsevaks tie this sacred thread to each other after the *Shakha* ends. Over the last several decades, the RSS has expanded this programme in a very interesting manner. After tying sacred thread to each other, the Swayamsevaks go to the nearby slums, *Jhuggi-Jhonpri* clusters or habitats where the poor and the underserved live and tie *Rakhi* to the residents living there.

□

6
The *Pracharak*

A full-time volunteer in the RSS is known as *Pracharak*. The life of a *Pracharak* is based on celibacy, dedication and commitment. Generally those who have attended three major training camps of the RSS known as, *Sangh Shiksha Varga*, are deputed as *Pracharak*.

Some of the full-time volunteers in the RSS are also known as *Vistarak*. The difference between a *Vistarak* and a *Pracharak* is that the *Vistarak* spends upto one year as a full-time volunteer while the *Pracharak* has an experience of more than one year as a full-timer.

Currently, there are around 4,000 *Pracharaks* who work in RSS and several of its frontal organisations. A *pracharak* doesn't marry. Though, in some of the 'social service', projects in rural and tribal areas, the RSS has successfully experimented with a concept where married couple also work as full-time volunteers.

A blog post by one of the RSS *Pracharaks* (http://indiantake.blogspot.in) aptly describes the profile of a RSS *Pracharak*.

RSS *Pracharak*

Work:

1. Start new *Shakhas.*
2. Improve the existing *Shakhas.*
3. Bring new people to *Shakhas.*
4. Spread RSS' ideology (nationalism).

Salary: Rs. Zero.

Facilities:

1. Food, clothing, shelter.
2. Basic expenses (soap, paste, etc.).
3. Travel expenses (bus, train, etc.).

Location: Anywhere in India.

Duration: As long as you wish.

Marital status: Single.

The senior positions in the RSS and its affiliate organisations are generally manned by the *Pracharaks.* The importance of the *Pracharaks* can be gauged from the fact that the two Prime Ministers produced by the Bharatiya Janata Party—Atal Bihari Vajpayee and Narendra Modi

have been RSS *Pracharaks*. The all-powerful post of 'General Secretary (organisation)', in all state units of the BJP as well as at the national level is entrusted to an RSS *Pracharak* only.

The life of a *Pracharak* is challenging. They stay in the RSS office and travel extensively to expand the ideology of the Sangh. Even the seniormost *Pracharaks* submit their travel bills diligently and get them reimbursed. They travel with the cheapest possible means of travel and make do with only a couple of dresses. They get up early in the morning before dawn and sleep late in the night working for 16-20 hours everyday for the organisational work. They are paid a basic stipend to take care of their day-to-day expenses which is less than the pocket money of a city-bred average Indian teenager.

Most of the *Pracharaks* prefer to have their meals at the homes of Swayamsevaks. This helps them to connect with larger number of people. Many *Pracharaks* spend a few years as full-time volunteers and then go back to the normal life. They get married, earn their livelihood by working somewhere or starting a business and remain connected with the RSS lifelong. No one is stopped, cajoled or pursued to stop being a *Pracharak*. The decision is absolutely based on the free will of an individual.

The concept of *Pracharak* has its roots in the early years of the RSS. After it was established in 1925, initially the RSS founder Dr. Hedgewar was the only full-time volunteer. He used to travel extensively to expand the activities of the RSS by starting new *Shakhas*.

As the RSS' work started expanding, on certain occasions, some senior colleagues of Dr. Hedgewar also started visiting certain areas and *Shakhas* to interact with the Swayamsevaks and other potential recruits there.

Initially, some of the college students who had become Swayamsevaks were sent during their summer break to the Vidarbha and Mahakaushal area. They spent around four-six weeks there and started the RSS *Shakhas*. They were called *Vistarak*.

Till 1932, the word *Pracharak* was not officially used in the RSS. Most of the Swayamsevaks were very young, only a few like Babasaheb Apte and Dadarao Parmarth were of much older age. Apte used to work in an insurance company in Nagpur. Parmarth had an excellent command over English language and was a highly motivational speaker. The RSS expanded its reach initially in districts like Wardha and Bhandara in Maharashtra where several *Shakhas* had started attracting the youth and the children.

There was an increasing need for Swayamsevaks who could spend few days in the places where new *Shakhas* were set-up. Dr. Hedgewar used to travel extensively himself and personally guided the work at most of these places but with rapid expansion of the RSS, it was becoming difficult for him to reach everywhere. Some of the elder Swayamsevaks started visiting the areas where new *Shakhas* were set up. They used to stay there for a few days and then come back to Nagpur.

Dr. Hedgewar often used to get letters from villages, towns and cities where several individuals used to urge him to start a *Shakha* at their native places. They needed someone experienced to come there and do the spadework in initial stages for setting up *Shakhas*. An assurance was always there in these messages that the basic needs of food, clothing, shelter, etc. would be taken care of if anyone agreed to come and start a *Shakha* at a new place.

Thus, the need for full-time RSS workers was discussed quite frequently among Dr. Hedgewar and some of the fellow Swayamsevaks. By 1932, senior RSS workers Dadarao Parmath, Babasaheb Apte, Rambhau Jamgade and Gopalrao Yerkuntwar had expressed their strong desire to work full-time to expand the RSS outreach.

In the second half of 1932, they became full-time workers of the RSS and were sent to different parts of the Maharashtra to carry forward the RSS work. Parmath went to Pune, Yerkuntwar went to Sangli (Maharashtra) and Jamgade was deputed for Yavatmal. They comprised the first batch of RSS *Pracharaks* and Dr. Hedgewar delivered an emotional address at a small function organised to formally start the tradition of becoming an RSS *Pracharak*. The robust tradition of becoming RSS *Pracharak* attracted many young and talented men in the years to come.

The RSS' work expanded in other parts of the country in 1930s with *Pracharaks* playing an important role. By

1937, in addition to several parts of Maharashtra, Swayamsevaks had started attending the RSS *Shakhas* at Mahakaushal in Madhya Pradesh and Benares (Varanasi) in Uttar Pradesh.

By this time, the need was felt to expand the RSS' work to Punjab, Delhi and other parts of the country. Dr. Hedgewar devised a unique and very effective strategy to meet this requirement. Those young Swayamsevaks in Nagpur who wanted to go out of the city for higher studies were motivated to go to those areas where new *Shakhas* were to be started. While studying they would also work for the RSS. Thus, under a well-planned strategy, Bhaurao Deoras (brother of third RSS Chief, Balasaheb Deoras), went to Lucknow in Uttar Pradesh to pursue B.Com. and LL.B. Krishna Joshi chose Sialkot (pre-partition Punjab) to take up his higher studies, Digambar Paturkar went to Lahore (pre-partition Punjab) and Moreshwar Munje went to Rawalpindi.

Meanwhile another group of college students opted to become *Pracharaks* after finishing their college education in Nagpur. This group comprised Vasantrao Oak, who went to Delhi and Bapurao Divakar, Narhari Parkhi and Mukundrao Munje who went to Patna, Danapur and Munger respectively in Bihar. Narayan Tarte was stationed in Gwalior (Madhya Pradesh) as a *Pracharak*.

Tarte deeply influenced a teenager in Gwalior, who later on became the Prime Minister of India. Atal Bihari Vajpayee, the first Swayamsevak to become the Prime Minister of India, recalls, "A *Pracharak*, Shri Narayanrao Tarte had come from Nagpur to start the *Shakha*. He was indeed a superb human being; a very simple man, a thinker and an expert organiser. What I am today is the making of Shri Tarte. Next to him I was inspired by Deendayal Upadhyaya and Bhaurao Deoras." Vajpayee himself was so deeply influenced by the RSS *Pracharaks* in his formative years that he gave up his studies in 1947 to become an RSS *Pracharak*.

In 1938, Eknath Ranade, who played an instrumental role in setting up the Vivekananda Rock Memorial and Vivekananda Kendra, whose birth centenary was celebrated in 2014, chose to become *Pracharak*. In a function at New Delhi in November 2014, Prime Minister Narendra Modi paid tribute to Ranade who had become a legend during his lifetime by performing the amazing feat of setting up of the Vivekanada Rock Memorial worth millions of rupees by taking contribution of one rupee each from millions of Indians and, hence, connecting them the task of nation-building.

Modi, while paying a tribute to him, said, "It was my good fortune that I had a chance to hold his finger and learn. He never compromised on perfection. There was not even one among us from the Sangh who was a perfectionist like him."

"I used to sit in the discussions that used to take place on the statue. Eknathji was very particular about the direction in which the statue would face and the scene that would be visible from the eyes of Vivekananda. He ensured the rocks were strong and would not crumble, and the chemical coating would preserve the statue. I learnt planning and looking ahead from him," Modi said.

Ranade, after finishing his post-graduation, went to Jabalpur (Madhya Pradesh) as a *Pracharak* in 1938. Modi, who witnessed his simplicity first-hand, says about Ranade, "He encouraged youth that just being inspired by Swami Vivekananda Ji is not enough, we must live like him. He established a memorial worth millions but himself lived in a small room, terrace of which was made of tin. Eknathji always did things keeping the future in mind and, in a simple manner, he believed every work should be done with public participation."

In 1939, Vithalrao Patki went to Kolkata as a *Pracharak*. The RSS expanded its outreach in Southern part of the country also with Janardan Chinchalkar reaching Madras to start the RSS *Shakhas*.

The list of *Pracharaks*, who have had significant influence on the socio-economic and political discourse of this country, is almost endless. To name a few, Pandit Deendayal Upadhyaya, who defined the theory of integral humanism which is the bed-rock of BJP's ideological frame-work, Dattopant Thengadi, an organiser *par excellence* and a brilliant strategist and thinker who founded India's largest trade union Bharatiya Mazdoor Sangh (BMS), Nanaji Deshmukh who played a pivotal role in forging an alliance under the leadership of Jayprakash Narayan and was one of the key architects of Janata Party Government in 1977. He later on set up Deendayal Research Institute and did phenomenal work in the area of self-sustainable holistic development in rural India, setting up new models of success. A galaxy of political leaders of BJP has followed the tradition of being an RSS *Pracharak* including current Prime Minister of India Narendra Modi. All the RSS Chiefs have been *Pracharaks*. The top brass of the RSS and heads of almost all the frontal

organisations have also followed the hallowed tradition of being an RSS *Pracharak*.

While most of the RSS *Pracharaks* often work for the organisation and the society till they breathe last, there are many who at times fall sick due to old age or do not remain mobile. The RSS takes care of them. Right from their treatment to their last rites, are being taken care of by the RSS. They are held in high esteem and all the functionaries and Swayamsevaks remain in touch with them. This becomes possible as the feeling of being, 'one family', is imbibed in the Swayamsevaks and, hence, the older *Pracharaks* may not be actively working but they are treated as elders in the family.

□

7
Training Camps: Sangh Shiksha Varga

The RSS conducts several training camps to strengthen its organisation. These camps can be broadly classified into four categories:

1. Sangh Shiksha Varga - First Year.
2. Sangh Shiksha Varga - Second Year.
3. Sangh Shiksha Varga - Third Year.
4. Sheet Shivir (Winter Camp).

A day at these camps typically begins at four in the morning and ends at ten in the night. The morning and evening hours are used for physical exercises. The afternoons and late evening hours are used for intellectual discourses and discussions on various ideological issues as well as contemporary developments in the context of the ideological framework.

The food served during these camps is vegetarian and without spice. It is cooked by the Swayamsevaks and served by them. Every camp begins and ends with surgical precision. Every activity is pre-planned and there is self-discipline. These camps are residential and Swayamsevaks sleep in dormitories.

While the first and second year camps as well as the winter camps are organised at the provincial and sometimes district levels, the third-year camp is organised at the RSS headquarters at Nagpur. The 'Third-Year' camp is the most coveted one and selected Swayamsevaks from all over the country attend it. It is a 30-day camp and organised during the summers and hence admist the soaring heat in Nagpur in Maharashtra. This training camp can only be attended by those who have attended the first-and the second-year camps. Generally, young men above the age of 16 years attend the first-and second-year camps while the third-year camp is attended by Swayamsevaks above 18 years of age. A large number of Swayamsevaks, who attend the third-year camp mostly choose to become a *Pracharak*. However, not everyone finishing the third-year camp does that.

All the Swayamsevaks who attend the camp pay a nominal fee that collectively takes care of the expenses incurred for the camp.

According to the annual progress report of the RSS presented in the meeting of Akhil Bharatiya Pratinidhi Sabha at Bangalore in March 2014:

"During the year 2013-2014, all over the country, in all, 48 first-year common Sangh Shiksha Vargs, 6 first-year special Sangh Shiksha Vargs, 12 second-year Sangh Shiksha Vargs, one common third-year Sangh Shiksha Varg, one third-year special Sangh Shiksha Varg were held, the total number of Vargs being 68. In the first-year common Varg a total of 10,435 Swayamsevaks from 6,759 places, and in the first-year special Varg, 386

Swayamsevaks from 286 places attended as trainees. In the second-year Vargs, 2,231 Swayamsevaks from 1,825 places attended as trainees. And in the third-year common Varg, 607 Swayamsevaks representing 565 places, and in the third-year special Varg, 360 Swayamsevaks participated as trainees."

The first RSS training camp was held at Nagpur in 1929. It was organised for 40 days from May 1 to June 10. Initially, these camps were called 'Summer Camps', as they were organised during the summer vacations. The name 'Sangh Shiksha Varg', was used after 1950 for these camps.

The training curriculum of the RSS for these camps has evolved gradually. In the early years of RSS, the focus during these training camps was primarily on 'March Past' and other military activities. A significant number of commands were given in English language.

B.N. Varadpande, a senior RSS functionary from Nagpur-recalls in his book, *Sangh Karyapaddhati Ka Vikas*: In one of the meetings, there was discussion about how we should address the summer camps which were being organised. Someone suggested the name should be 'Training Classes'. Another Swayamsevak added that as these camps are to expand the RSS *Shakhas*, so we should call it Sangh Training Class. Dr. (Hedgewar) said that as these camps are organised to prepare workers for the RSS which can give maximum amount of time to the organisation, so it should be called, 'Officers' Training Camp (OTC).

OTC remains a popular word for the RSS training camps even today, though it is no more the official name of the RSS camp. *Guruji*, who was the second RSS Chief, re-named these camps as *Sangh Shiksha Varg*.

Upto 1937, there used to be some entertainment programmes in the RSS camps on Saturday evening and on Sunday, the daily routine of programmes for the *Shakha* were also not followed. However, this 'break' was shelved after 1938 as it appeared that this affected the training programme. In days to come, the time-period of the camps was also reduced from 40 to 30 days.

Till 1934, the RSS camps were conducted only in Nagpur. The second-and third-year camps started at Pune

in 1935. In 1938, the first-and second-year camps were also started in Lahore.

There have been several interesting anecdotes related to the RSS training camps, where class, creed, caste does not matter. All the trainees are treated as one and the same. There is no discrimination. It might look quite ordinary today but it was an extraordinary feat to bring trainers and trainees from all castes together and make them eat together and stay together as brothers.

In 1934, Mahatma Gandhi visited a Sangh Shiksha Varg at Wardha. While addressing the RSS workers, he recalled during one of his speeches in Delhi on September 16, 1947. "I visited the RSS camp years ago, when the founder, Shri Hedgewar was alive. I was very much impressed by your discipline, the complete absence of untouchability and the rigorous simplicity. Since then, the Sangh has grown. I am convinced that any organisation, which is inspired by the high ideal of service and self-sacrifice, is bound to grow in strength."

Dr. Bhimrao Ambedkar visited Sangh Shiksha Varga in Pune in 1939. When Dr. Ambedkar asked

Dr. Hedgewar whether there were any untouchables in the camp, the RSS founder replied that there were neither touchables nor untouchables, but only Hindus there. Dr. Ambedkar said, "I am surprised to find the Swayamsevaks moving about in absolute equality and brotherhood without even caring to know the caste of the others."

Leading freedom fighter Jayaprakash Narayan, a known socialist, who led the historic movement against the anti-democratic forces in 1970s, addressed an RSS training camp in Patna on November 3, 1977.

The RSS training camps are organised not only in India but abroad also where the organisation works under different names, such as Hindu Swayamsevak Sangh. In addition to the *Sangh Shiksha Varga*, the short-term training camps are also organised by the RSS in India as well as abroad. However, within the Sangh Parivar, winter camps are one of the oldest and the most popular training camps.

The first winter camp was organised in 1928 at Nagpur near Sonegaon Airport. It was an open space. This could also be termed as the first training camp of RSS. These are generally for shorter duration of around a week and are organised during winters. Even Swayamsevaks below 16 years of age can also attend them. The routine remains the same where they get up at four in the morning

and sleep at ten in the night. They are generally organised during December vacations.

There is no excuse for anyone to skip the tight schedule that binds all in a much stronger bond of brotherhood and a better ideological perspective along with confidence that comes out with strong focus on building up their physical strength. The aim is to build men of character who have the physical prowess and mental strength to face any adversity.

During all the RSS training camps, Swayamsevaks sleep on the floor, personal belongings are not kept in lock and key, the security of the camp venue is also being taken care of by the Swayamsevaks with round the clock vigil. The senior Swayamsevaks from the nearby areas are entrusted with various arrangements and these camps are generally organised in a school or college building. The RSS-affiliated organisations now run thousands of educational institutions. So the space is now readily available for the RSS camps.

Everyone is not allowed to attend these camps. The trainees which are selected are often screened at the *Shakha* level and the senior RSS functionaries identify the Swayamsevaks which have greater potential to dedicate themselves completely for the Sangh work. They are motivated and encouraged to attend these camps. There is no compulsion to attend the training camps for anyone but a large number of Swayamsevaks attend these camps and come back with much greater ideological commitment to work for the cause.

The RSS has organised some of the biggest training camps with 22,000 Swayamsevaks attending a camp in Karnataka while in 1988, more than 35,000 Swayamsevaks attended a training camp at Taljai near Pune.

One of the prime purposes of these training camps is to ensure that the top RSS ideologues and stalwarts can deliver lectures to Swayamsevaks coming from different parts of the districts, states and the country at one place. It is one of the most effective ways for the senior RSS functionaries to connect with the Swayamsevaks. There are no political discussions in any of the RSS training camps, the focus is on ideology, physical strength, character-building, organisational work and key national challenges.

□

8
The Prayer

Everyday all the RSS *Shakhas* end up with a prayer which is recited by all the Swayamsevaks present at the venue of the *Shakha*. The Swayamsevaks stand in columns and rows in attention at the place where the RSS *Shakha* is taking place, one person recites the prayer and the rest of the Swayamsevaks repeat the lines with their right hand in a position similar to the that, which they take while entering the *Shakha* and bowing their head to the Saffron Flag. The right palm is parallel to the ground with the thumb of the same hand touching solar plexus.

In addition to the daily *Shakha*, all the major programmes of the RSS wind up formally with the recital of the RSS prayer. Most of the Swayamsevaks know it by heart. The RSS prayer is in Sanskrit and is considered to be very sacred by the Swayamsevaks as it is an explicit tribute to the motherland. As one traverses through the meaning of the prayer, one realises that by reciting these lines everyday, the objective is to strengthen the feeling of nationalism among the Swayamsevaks. Given below is the text of the prayer and its meaning:

"Namaste sada vatsale matribhume
Twaya hindubhume shukham vardhitoham

Mahamangale punyabhume twadarthe
Patatwesha kayo namaste namaste ‖ 1 ‖

Prabho shaktiman hindurashtrangabhuta
Ime sadaram twam namamovayam
Twadiyao karyao baddha katiyam
Shubhamashisham dehi tatpurtaye |

Ajayam cha vishwasya dehisha shaktim
Sushilam jagad jena namra vabet

Shrutam chaiva yat kantakakirnamargam
Swayam swikritam nah sugam karyayet || 2 ||
Shamutkarshanihshreyasasaikamugram
Param sadhanam naam veerabratam
Tadantahsphuratwakshwa dheyanishtha
Hridantah prajagartu teebrahnisham |
Bijetree cha nah sanhata karyashaktir
Vidhayasya dharmasya sanrakshanam
Param vaibhavam netumetat swarashtram
Samartha vabatwashisha te vrisham || 3 ||

Bharat Mata ki jay ||"

Though there have been many interpretations of the RSS prayer in English, but the most appropriate one has been provided by the second RSS *Sarsanghchalak* Madhav Sadashivrao Golwalkar. Here is the interpretation/ meaning of the RSS Prarthana according to *Guru* Golwalkar:

"Forever I bow to thee, O Loving Motherland! O Motherland of us Hindus, Thou hast brought me up in happiness. May my life, O great and blessed Holy Land, be laid down in Thy Cause. I bow to Thee again and again.

We the children of the Hindu Nation bow to Thee in reverence, O Almighty God. We have girded up our loins to carry on Thy work. Give us Thy Holy blessings for its fulfilment. O Lord! Grant us such might as no power on earth can ever challenge such purity of character as would command the respect of the whole world and such knowledge as would make easy the thorny path that we have voluntarily chosen.

May we be inspired with the spirit of stern heroism, that is sole and ultimate means of attaining the highest spiritual bliss with the greatest temporal prosperity. May intense and everlasting devotion to our ideal ever enthuse our hearts. May our victorious organised power of action, by Thy Grace, be wholly capable of protecting our dharma and leading this nation of ours to the highest pinnacle of glory."

The evolution of the RSS prayer is significant to understand that every tradition in the RSS has evolved with active participation of the Swayamsevaks. The RSS is not rigid about even the most sacrosanct of its traditions and is ready to change with time.

Though the RSS was founded in 1925, but the present-day *Prarthana* or 'Prayer' came into existence only in 1940. There is an interesting piece of history that provides a peep into the thinking and collective decision-making process within the country.

Till 1940, the RSS prayer comprised two *shlokas* –one in Hindi and the other one in Marathi. During the first 15 years, the RSS had established its presence in almost all the provinces across the country. Several young men had become full-time workers and moved to different areas to expand the presence of the RSS.

With rapid expansion of the organisation, the need for a simple prayer in Sanskrit was increasingly felt. Incidentally, several instructions on the RSS *Shakhas* for conducting various programmes were also given primarily in Marathi and English till 1940. The need for having an instruction manual in Sanskrit was also felt as Sanskrit was one language which could be spoken across the nation.

To discuss these issues, a meeting was convened in February 1939 at a place called Sindi, around 50 km away from Nagpur. It was organised at the residence of a senior RSS functionary Nanasaheb Talatule. The RSS founder Dr. Hedgewar, *Guru* Golwalkar, Bala Saheb Deoras, Appaji Joshi, Vithalrao Patki, Talatule, Tatyarao Telang, Babaji Salodkar and Krishnarao Mohril participated in the meeting. The arrangements for the meeting were looked after by Babanrao Pandit.

Several important decisions, which had a long-lasting impact on the way RSS functioned, were taken at this

meeting. These decisions had a definitive influence on the structure of the RSS.

Those who attended the meeting conducted a detailed review of the way RSS functioned from 1925 to 1939 and decided to bring uniformity. Marathi and English were replaced by Sanskrit as a medium of instruction. It was decided that the instructions issued at the RSS *Shakhas* would be in Sanskrit henceforth. The issue of developing an RSS prayer in Sanskrit was also discussed. The essence of the prayer was initially penned in Marathi and then the *Karyavah* (Head) of Mohite *Shakha* at Nagpur, Narayanrao Bhide, who was known to be an expert of Sanskrit language, was entrusted with the responsibility of converting the Marathi prose into a Sanskrit prayer. He did his job so well that, with hardly any changes, the Sanskrit translation was accepted by all. For the first time, this Sanskrit prayer was recited in the RSS' camp held at Pune in the presence of Dr. Hedgewar and *Guru* Golwalkar. The same Sanskrit prayer is recited even today in the RSS *Shakhas* without any change.

Till 1940, several English words were used to carry out routine activities on daily *Shakhas*, such as Formation, March-Past, Advance in Review Order, Line Formation, Halt, Form Fours, Band, Bugle, Flute, Side Drum, etc. Both Bhide and Salodkar worked to develop an exhaustive instruction manual in Sanskrit. All these instructions developed in 1940 in Sanskrit have been in use ever since.

□

9

The RSS Uniform: From Khaki Shorts to Brown Pants

One of the distinct features of the RSS has been the uniform of Swayamsevaks. It should be made clear here, before we proceed further to discuss this subject, that the Swayamsevaks are not expected to wear this uniform every day.

Only on some special occasions such as the RSS festivals or the annual address by the RSS Chief or when a get together of many shakhas is held, the full uniform is to be donned by swayamsevaks attending it.

When the RSS started its journey in 1925 the official uniform of the RSS comprised Khaki baggy shorts, Khaki shirt, long boots, Khaki cap shaped like a rhombus. Since then several changes have been made in the uniform which is known as 'Ganvesh' within the organisation.

Ganvesh is a word which is commonly used in Hindi as well as Sanskrit language. Ganvesh is a combination of two words: 'Gan' (which means a structured set of people) and 'vesh' (which means) 'attire'. Hence the term 'Ganvesh' is used for the official dress or uniform of the RSS swayamsevaks.

Over the last 90 years following changes have been brought in the RSS uniform:

- Khaki shirt was changed to white shirt
- Khaki cap was replaced by black cap.
- Long boots were replaced by simple black canvas shoes with laces
- Leather belt was replaced by the plastic belt.
- Last but not the least, the most visible and well known symbol of the RSS-Khaki shorts- was replaced in 2016 by brown pants.

The last decision has been a monumental one and also indicated the RSS' will to bring change within the organisation to meet the new challenges. The Khaki baggy shorts have been understood to be a deterrent to attract younger people to the RSS shakhas. The issue had been flagged several times over the last several years and the discussion went on.

After threadbare discussion, the RSS finally went ahead with the decision to replace Khaki shorts with brown pants. Making the announcement in March 2016, the RSS General Secretary Bhaiyyaji Joshi said, "We have decided to replace khaki shorts with brown-coloured full pants (RSS uniform)...." Trousers are more common in normal life. We are the people who move with times. So we had no hesitation to change dress code."

The decision was officially taken at the Akhil Bhartiya Pratinidhi Sabha meeting held at Nagaur (Rajasthan) March, 2016. "Any mass organisation cannot grow without a change. The RSS has always brought changes to stay in sync with the times," RSS spokesperson Manmohan

Vaidya told reporters in Nagaur after the decision was announced.

The RSS uniform is generally not available in the open market. It is sold in the RSS offices at a nominal price which just covers the cost. These uniforms are available in all sizes and are sold on "No Profit, No loss" principle. Anyone can go to their nearest RSS office where these uniforms are available and can buy them.

□

10

Guruji: The Second RSS Chief

Madhavrao Sadashivrao Golwalkar was the second *Sarsanghchalak* of the RSS. He is commonly known in Sangh parleys as *Guruji*. This name was initially used by his students in Banaras Hindu University where he used to teach.

His father's name was Sadashivrao who was a teacher and his mother was Lakshmibai. They lived in Nagpur. In his childhood, he was also called 'Madhu' lovingly. Nagpur was a province of modern Madhya Pradesh when Golwalkar was born there. Although his mother tongue was Marathi but as his father was posted frequently in Hindi-speaking areas, so Madhu had good command over Hindi. He was equally good in English too.

H.V. Seshadri recalled in a biographical sketch, "Madhavrao was a sharp boy with prodigious memory.

Once his school teacher Prof. Gardener was teaching the Bible. Madhavrao interrupted saying, "Sir, the reference given by you is not correct. Actually it should have been like this...." And saying thus. he uttered another sentence. All the students and Prof. Gardener were amazed. But when it was cross-checked with the Bible, he was found to be correct. At the end of the class, the Professor gave him a fond pat on the back. This incident served as a witness to his qualities like exceptional memory, courage and unshakable self-confidence. His memory served him till his last day. Even today, throughout the country, people recall anecdotes of his phenomenal memory."

Madhavrao completed his intermediate studies in 1924 and went to Banaras Hindu University to do B.Sc. Seshadri recounts another interesting anecdote that provides glimpse to Guruji's some lesser known extraordinary aspects during his younger days, "The huge repository of invaluable books in the library there was as if waiting to quench his thirst for knowledge. Madhavrao started reading the books, through and through, one by one. One day his toe was bitten by a scorpion, but he very casually cut that portion of his foot, dipped that foot in potassium permanganate solution and resumed his study. Amazed at this, one of his friends asked, "How do you manage to study despite such severe pain?" Madhavrao replied, "Well, the scorpion has bitten my foot, not my mind!" Later on also, people have many a times witnessed his tranquil tolerance under most excruciating physical pains."

He returned to Nagpur after completing his Masters in Zoology with first class and a few months later, opted to go for research in Chennai. In 1929, as his father retired from the service, it resulted in financial stress on the family. Madhavrao had to leave his research work and return to Nagpur.

Madhavrao began teaching at Banaras Hindu University (BHU) from August 1931. He was a popular teacher among students. He was known for providing financial assistance and textbooks for needy students. More than often he ended up spending a significant part of his salary to help students. Pandit Madan Mohan Malaviya, Founder of BHU, was fond of him.

Golwalkar came in contact with the RSS through a Swayamsevak from Nagpur, Bhaiyyaji Dani, who was sent there as a student by Dr. Hedgewar. He became the *Palak* (Guardian) of that *Shakha*. After finishing his term at BHU, *Guruji* returned to Nagpur and completed his study of law.

In Nagpur, Dr. Hedgewar was constantly in touch with Golwalkar and motivated him to get increasingly involved with the RSS. In 1934, he was appointed as *Sarvadhikari* (officer-in-charge) of *Sangh Shiksha Varga* (Officer's Training Camp) in Akola.

By now, his parents had started thinking about his marriage. Seshadri recounts, "Shri Guruji's mother put forth the proposal for his marriage and said if he decided against marrying, their Golwalkar family lineage would cease to exist – he being the only surviving son. Shri Guruji replied, "In the present situation, it is necessary that, for the welfare of the society, if the family lineages of not only me but several others like me are terminated, I am not in the least worried." The debate over his marriage ended then and there."

Meanwhile, Golwalkar came in contact with Sri Ramakrishna Ashram's Swami Bhaskareshvarananda in Nagpur. There he became close to Sri Amitabh Maharaj and told him that Swami Akhandananda, a direct disciple of revered Sri Ramakrishna Paramahansa, was staying at the Sargachi Ashram in the then Bengal.

He quietly left for Sargachi in search of a spiritual guide in 1936. In Sargachi, he immersed himself in the service of Swami Akhandananda, who was quite old and indisposed.

After six months, Swamiji decided to initiate him into the Order. The experience was overwhelming as he himself described, "I have received the blessings one gets after innumerable births. My body felt thrilled all over and I am finding myself an altogether changed person."

In February 1937, the revered Swamiji passed away after which Golwalkar spent some time in Ramakrishna Ashram, Belur Math. Then along with Amitabh Maharaj, he returned to Nagpur.

In Nagpur, Golwalkar found his right calling and immersed himself in organisational work of the RSS from 1938 under the mentorship of Dr. Hedgewar. Golwalkar explained it later, "Like spirituality, organization of the Nation has towards it my inclination from early days. I believe that I would be in a better position to achieve it successfully being a part of the Sangh. Hence, I have dedicated myself to the activities of the Sangh. In the light of the insight and practical approach of Swami Vivekananda, I think my decision is appropriate."

In 1940, after the death of Dr. Hedgewar, he became the *Sarsanghchalak*. For the next 30 years, he covered the country twice travelling to almost every nook and corner of the country relentlessly to expand the footprints of the RSS. Most of the frontal organisations of the RSS came into existence during his tenure as the RSS Chief.

According to Seshadri, "It was but natural that this superhuman effort and hard work of Shri Guruji would finally take its toll on his health. By the time Shri Guruji turned 60, his health started deteriorating. In May 1970, a lump was noticed in his chest. It was diagnosed to be cancerous. Even then he decided to get it treated only after his already scheduled tour of May and June was completed."

Dr. Praful Desai, who operated upon him at Tata Cancer Hospital, was not an RSS worker. But he wrote, "I was wondering how Shri Guruji would be able to take such an intense and long surgery at 65. But the calmness, courage and cooperation with which he went through the whole procedure, with the smile never leaving his face, it was amazing. He started walking around the very next day." He lost no time in getting back to his gruelling schedule and started travelling extensively again.

Meanwhile, by the end of 1971, he started feeling seriously unwell. Seshadri recalls an intimate discussion and an interesting incident in the history of the RSS at this juncture when the issue of changing the name of organisation was discussed. "He (Golwalkar) felt, his end was nearing. He decided to have his last discussions with the prominent Swayamsevaks as per the Hindu tradition. Accordingly, in the Tatvajnana Vidyapeeth at Thane in Maharashtra, run by honourable (now late) Pandurang Shastri Athawale ji, the programme was organized. Shri Guruji was present during the *Abhyas Varg* (study camp) of the prominent workers deployed in various activities aimed at narturing the true national spirit. There were suggestions that if the Sangh adopted the word *Bharatiya* instead of *Hindu*, it would absolve it of the charge that it was communal. Shri Guruji presented the Hindu thought in its positive aspect and removed all the doubts on this issue with reasoning based on historic perspective and his personal experience. Along with this, he also discussed indepth other ideologies and did a comparative study of other belief systems and elaborately explained how the Hindu philosophy alone is capable of ensuring the highest standard of welfare for the humanity and yield permanent happiness."

On March 25, 1973, he addressed members of the Akhil Bharatiya Pratinidhi Sabha at Nagpur attended by the most important functionaries of the RSS from all over the country. He had to struggle hard to speak but he still managed to speak for 40 minutes. He said, "The single aim of all our different endeavours should be to make our nation stand high commanding worldwide respect for our country."

"Whatever be the atmosphere, tread on your path with this faith that the word 'Hindu' will be recognized all over one day." He concluded his speech saying, *Vijay Hi Vijay Hai* (ever victorious). This was his last public address. His health deteriorated further.

The way Golwalkar pushed his limits for the organisational cause almost became a legend and is still recalled on every possible occasion in the RSS by millions of Swayamsevaks. Seshadri has given an authentic account of his last few days. "In Nagpur, in May (1973), the Third Year Shiksha Varga of the Sangh was going on. It was impossible for Shri Guruji to make it to the Varga. Hence, in keeping with his strong urge, it was arranged that Swayamsevaks province-wise were called into the Sangh *Karyalaya* to meet him. There he got acquainted with them and emotionally appealed to them to carry on the Sangh work whole-heartedly and steadfast. The programme lasted from 16th May to 25th May. Later even that could not be carried on. The Swayamsevaks from various parts of the country and other eminent personalities from all walks of life kept pouring into the Sangh *Karyalaya* to enquire about his health. On the 3rd of June, when the *Sanchalika* of *Rashtra Sevika Samiti*, respected Mausi Kelkar called upon him, he meaningfully said, "I am fully ready." On the evening of 4th June, when the workers attending upon him came with a bottle of oil to give him massage, but it was empty. He jokingly said, "It's over now! Good. Tomorrow, who will be there for massage?" On 5th June in the morning, he took his bath and meditated sitting on his usual seat. Later at 9.30 in the night, he breathed his last and his soul got liberated from the shackles of the mortal body."

On the morning of June 6, three sealed letters, written by Golwalkar, were opened and read. The first letter was read by the *Sanghchalak* of Maharashtra province Babasaheb Bhide, which mentioned that Balasaheb Deoras was to be given the charge of *Sarsanghchalak* after Golwalkar. The other two letters were read by Balasaheb Deoras.

In the second letter, he had indicated that it was not desirable that a memorial be erected for anyone other than that of the founder of the Sangh, Dr. Hedgewar.

The third letter by Golwalkar read: "If I have ever knowingly or unknowingly caused hurt to anyone, to all of them I tender my apologies with folded hands."

A composition of Saint Tukaram was also mentioned in this letter:

"O Saints! Please forward my last request
To the God that He might not forget me.
He knows everything; what may I say more.
Tukaram says his head placed on His feet
I may always remain under the shadow of His grace."

His body was laid by the side of the memorial of Dr. Hedgewar in Reshambag, (Nagpur) on a pyre made of sandalwood. Later, the Saffron Flag of the RSS was hoisted and thousands of Swayamsevaks and others who gathered there recited the RSS prayer in grief-struck tone.

Seshadri comments appropriately, "Now Reshambag is home to two great personalities in their Chaitanya form. Dr. Hedgewar sitting in the form of his image is on the upper floor of Smriti-Mandir and Shri Guruji, like the sage Dadhichi (who sacrificed his body for the welfare of Gods and mankind), as a Smriti Chinha (a symbolic memory)." The statue of Dr. Hedgewar seems to be saying, "My selection was just right. Shri Guruji has spread the glory of the Sangh worldwide."

Tributes by the Nation

Acharya Vinoba Bhave said, "Shri Guruji was not in the least narrow-minded. He was always driven by the lofty ideals of national interests. He considered other religions like Christianity and Islam with due respect and always hoped that in Bharat nobody would be isolated."

Jagadguru Shankaracharya of Puri said, "He was a saint, in white robes."

Jain Acharya Sushil Kumar Muniji said, "Shri Guruji was a giant of a man of our heritage."

Jain Sage Acharya Tulasi said, "He was endowed with the qualities of both a connoisseur and a thinker."

The then Prime Minister, Indira Gandhi said in the Parliament, "We have lost in *Guru* Golwalkar a famous personality, who was not a Member of the Parliament. He held a respected position in the nation by the force of his personality and the intensity of his convictions."

Even ideological opponents extolled the virtues of Golwalkar.

Samar Guha, a Socialist leader, said, "He inspired the qualities of patriotism, dedication and service in thousands of youth of the country."

Another Socialist leader S.M. Joshi said, "Shri Guruji was a sage."

Lok Nayak Jai Prakash Narayan paid him a tribute by saying, "Shri Guruji was a spiritually great personality, who awakened thousands of youth to true nationalism."

Seshadri's conclusion about Golwalkar's work sums up the feelings of Swayamsevaks of the RSS about their second *Sarsanghchalak*, "As a harbinger of a new nationhood, Shri Guruji infused a unique intrinsic power into the national life through his unmatched personality and actions."

□

11
Balasaheb Deoras: The Third RSS Chief

Madhukar Dattatraya Deoras, commonly known as Balasaheb Deoras, was born on December 11, 1915 in Nagpur, Maharashtra to Dattatraya Krishnarao Deoras and Parvathibai. His brother Bhaurao Deoras was also a *Pracharak* and senior functionary of the RSS.

Balasaheb was educated in New English High School. He matriculated from Berar Board of Secondary Education of the Central Provinces in 1931.

Then he took admission in Moris College (now Nagpur Mahavidyalaya). He graduated from the same college and later completed LL.B. degree in College of Law, Nagpur University. He was associated with the RSS right since its inception.

Inspired by Dr. Hedgewar, Balasaheb decided to devote his life for the RSS and became a *Pracharak*. His first stint, as a *Pracharak*, was in the pre-partition Bengal.

He was appointed as the *Sahsarkaryavaha* (Joint General Secretary) of the RSS in 1946. In 1965, he was elevated to the position of the *Sarkaryavah* (General Secretary). After the demise of the second RSS Chief, Guruji, he became the *Sarsanghchalak* on June 5, 1973.

Balasaheb's family hailed from Andhra Pradesh but was settled in Nagpur. He had three siblings – one brother and two sisters. One of the major contributions of the Third RSS Chief was his crusade against untouchability. His declaration, made in 1974, that, "If untouchability is not wrong, nothing in the world is wrong", fired the imagination of Swayamsevaks and provide a great fillip to the national efforts to fight the menace of untouchability, a major curse of the Indian social system.

An organiser *par excellence*, he led the spectacular fight against Emergency, imposed by the then Prime Minister Indira Gandhi. The RSS was banned by Gandhi but under Balasaheb's dynamic and pragmatic leadership, the RSS led the fight against this draconian step from the front despite being put behind bars like several other leaders.

Political commentator Muzaffar Hussain wrote in newspaper article in 1996, "Indian politics experienced its first internal upheaval with the declaration of the Emergency in June 1975. This was the second time RSS was banned during Deoras' career and the first for him to face in his capacity as the *Sarsanghchalak*. The whole of India was turned into a veritable jail. I need not repeat what the Sangh had to go through. Balasaheb, however, gave it a positive turn. While in jail, he had the opportunity to react with the leaders and activists of many banned Muslim organisations including the Jamaat-e-Islami. As a result, the two parties came closer not only in their thinking and responses but also in their day-to-day dealings. By their conduct, the RSS Adhikaris dispelled the Muslims' apprehension that the RSS was their enemy. It was the first miracle Balasaheb achieved by giving a positive turn to the Muslim perception of the Sangh. After being acquainted with the ideology of the RSS, hitherto dubbed a body of militant Hindus, leaders of the Jamaat-e-Islami came to conclusion that, barring image-worship. There was no fundamental difference in Islam and Sanatan Dharma. The jail during the Emergency became a turning point where the impasse between the two communities came to an end and paved the way for a dialogue."

An online article published in 2012 at one of the RSS affiliated websites explained working style of Balasaheb Deoras: "Gifted with a profoundly critical intellect, Balasaheb gave a much-needed fillip to the process of a direct dialogue with workers at different levels. He himself would sit for long hours seeking answers to a number of doubts arising in the minds of Swayamsevaks. This two-way intellectual feedback proved very useful in firming up the conviction of the rank and file of the Sangh Parivar. Such an organisational direction was particularly needed in view of the fast-changing intellectual agenda at the national level, with the phenomenal rise of Hindu awareness and Hindutva coming up to centre stage."

Balasaheb continued as Sarsanghachalak till 1994 after which he stepped down due to ill health paving the way for Prof. Rajendra Singh to replace him. For the first time in the RSS, a *Sarsanghachalak had announced a successor when alive. Earlier the practice was of a 'will' being made public posthumously.*

After continuous deterioration in health, Deoras passed away on 17 June 1996.

□

12

Rajju Bhaiya: The Fourth RSS Chief

On July 19, 2003, Swami Chinmayananda Union Minister of State of Home Affairs in the Atal Behari Vajpayee-led NDA government wrote in English daily *The Pioneer*, "I was to learn of the sad demise of Rajju Bhaiya on July 14, 2003. It was not easy for me. The way he discharged his important responsibilities as a teacher, *Pracharak*, and RSS *Sarsanghchalak*, with straightforwardness and simplicity, and inspired crores of Indians for a long

time, will always be remembered. As an individual, many of my emotional memories are linked with him. Today it seems quite expedient that while paying my homage to him, I should share my experiences with the public."

Swamiji has summed up the long and fruitful life of Rajju Bhaiya very well in this obituary. Prof. Rajendra Singh, popularly called Rajju Bhaiya, was born in Bulandshahar, Uttar Pradesh on January 29, 1922. His father Balbir Singh was the first Indian to be selected for the Indian Engineering Service.

Rajju Bhaiya received his primary education in Nainital; later, he studied in the Allahabad University. He was a student of Physics and Atomic Science was his special subject. His post-graduation answer papers were checked by Indian Nobel Laureate Dr. C.V. Raman.

It is said that Dr. Raman was so impressed with his answers that he invited him to do research under him. Meanwhile, he also received an invitation for the appointment to the post of lecturer. Instead of accepting the proposal of research, he accepted the post of lecturer and taught in the University of Allahabad up to 1965. In 1966, he became a *Pracharak* of the RSS.

Rajju Bhaiya always remained detached from all materialistic pleasures and, therefore, wanted nothing for himself. He used minimum possible clothes. Due to his nature, his father got a house constructed for him at Civil Lines, Allahabad, but he donated it to an educational institution, Saraswati Shishu Mandir.

It is also said that as his father and family members were probably under the impression that Rajju Bhaiya would donate whatever would be given to him for one of the social organisations, so he was not given any share of his paternal property.

According to Swami Chinmayananda, "He (Rajju Bhaiya) always kept aloof from his family. In Allahabad he lived in a room of the same Shishu Mandir. He spent most of his life in the offices of the Sangh. He was neither an account holder in any bank nor did he own even an inch of land. Simplicity of his nature and cordiality to everyone made him a man of his own style. In spite of his sincerity and complete dedication to the Sangh, he was liked by a large number of people in political parties. Working for the prestigious post of *Sarsanghchalak,* he was always cordial to all. Though physically he became sick, it never had any effect on his mind and intellect. He remained active till he was alive. He was always a supporter of education, Seva, Samarvata and harmony of thoughts. That is why, all the decisions taken by him as *Sarsanghchalak* helped the Sangh to widen its scope. His liberal thinking was widely supported. In spite of being a scholar of physics, his expression was always lucid."

Swami Chinmayananda recounts a very interesting personal experience, "During the Ayodhya movement in 1989, when we were arrested by the Mulayam Singh Government, Rajju Bhaiya, Mahant Avaidyanath and I were kept in the guest house of Jim Corbett Park. Though (Mulayam Singh)

Yadav had made high-level arrangements for the arrested persons, Rajju Bhaiya used to wash and dry his clothes himself and keep them under his pillow so that they would need no ironing. Being diabetic, he had to take insulin, but he used to inject it himself. Sometimes he used to prepare tea for everyone. Often in the evening he used to go for a walk. We accompanied him up to a long distance in the forests of Jim Corbett followed by the police. He used to laugh and say, "Brother! We and Mahantji are old and we cannot run. And Chinmayananda can't leave us alone. Then why are you following us?" When constables said they were following us to protect us from wild animals, he said, "Tigers do live here, but

you should know that tigers never attack tigers. All three of us are tigers and we don't need any kind of protection!"

Rajju Bhaiya was deeply spiritual. He is known to have always kept an edition of Sunderkand Gutka with him. It was presented to him by Brahmachari Prabhu Dattji Maharaj. It had a small picture of Lord Hanuman inside. "On November 30, 1989, when a programme of marching towards the Ram temple was made by the Karsevaks in Ayodhya, inspite of being in Jim Corbett, he advised me and Mahantji to observe a fast and read *Sunderkand* so that no untoward incident took place there. When the problem of finding a copy of Sunderkand in the forest came up, he took out his Gutka and gave us. We read Sunderkand keeping that picture of Lord Hanuman in front of us which he always preserved," recalled Swami Chinmayananda.

He was moved by the suffering of others and considered his duty to help them. Another incident recalled by Swami Chinmayananda reveals the emotional aspect of Rajju Bhaiya in this regard. "Once I was travelling with him to Bhagalpur by Vikramshila Express for the inauguration of a Saraswati Shishu Mandir. We were travelling in an AC coach; the lower berths were reserved for us. At night, both of us went to sleep on those berths. In the morning, when I woke up, I saw someone else sleeping on his berth; he was seated in a corner. When I wanted him to tell me about the new guest, he gestured me to remain silent. It so happened that, as per daily routine, when he woke up at 6.00 a.m., he went to the toilet and felt that someone was hanging by the door handle of the coach. It was winter. He opened the door and saw a boy of 9 or 10 shivering in the cold, somehow managing a toehold on the steps. He asked him in and made him sleep on his birth. On the way, he got some milk supplied from somewhere. He woke up the boy, opened the thermos and gave him hot milk to drink. When his followers came to meet him in Patna, he handed over that boy to them with instructions that after asking his address, arrangements be made to send him to his house."

On the first death anniversary of Rajju Bhaiya, the present RSS Chief Mohanrao Bhagwat, who was *Sarkaryavah* of the RSS at that time, provided one of the most insightful descriptions in an article titled "Sangh work first, I come later" in the RSS' weekly publication 'Organiser'.

"The prime qualities that Rajju Bhaiya had were to love all, treat all as his own, take everybody along with him, stay steadfast on truth, tell what is the truth and adopt simplicity. On the basis of these qualities, he had laid some principles of good behaviour, like treating all in the same manner. Without being influenced with age, status, eminence of a person, but treating each person as an individual, was his first principle. Many examples of this nature were seen in his life.

Once a Swayamsevak from a village of Chandrapur district in Maharashtra brought his younger brother for admission to a college in Pune. By then, Rajju Bhaiya had relinquished his duties as *Sarsanghchalak* to hand them over to Sudarshanji as he himself was recuperating his health at Kaushik Ashram. The *Vibhag Pracharak* of Chandrapur district had also given him a letter and telephone numbers of some prominent people.

The Swayamsevak reached Pune with his brother at 4 o'clock in the morning. He had come to Pune for the first time. On seeing their village outfits and style of talking when seeking the address, a tough-looking goonda began to stalk them. Both the brothers became frightened. They began making frantic phone calls to the local Sangh workers from a nearby telephone booth. Everyone who was contacted would invariably ask, "Where are you? Somehow or the other come to my house or reach the Sangh *Karyalaya* (RSS Office)." But they were terribly terrified, not knowing what to do. They were not able to tell even from which place they were calling. They even dialled the number of Kaushik Ashram. It was about 5.30 a.m. at that moment. Rajju Bhaiya himself picked up the phone. Without any fanfare, the Swayamsevak spoke out directly, "I am a Swayamsevak from Pipali village of Chandrapur district. I want to talk to Rajju Bhaiya."

Rajju Bhaiya replied, "Yes. Tell me what do you want, I am speaking."

The Swayamsevak explained the sequence of events concluding that the goonda was standing nearly and overhearing their talk. He was also preventing them from going anywhere. Rajju Bhaiya replied, "I can't even walk without any support, what help can I give you?" The Swayamsevak said he knew nothing about the city. Then, literally shouting on the phone, Rajju Bhaiya said, "You try to stall him there. I will send the police right now." Rajju Bhaiya had said this in such a loud tone that the goon standing close to the phone heard it and quietly slipped away.

Later, the Swayamsevak met Rajju Bhaiya and narrated the entire incident. If you look at it from the practical point of view, then you see that on one side was an ordinary Swayamsevak from an unknown village and on the other side was the former *Sarsanghchalak*, who was concerned for the Swayamsevak as an individual and not because he was big or small, a city-dweller, a village *Karyavah* or a *Sarkaryavah*.

Why did he do this? He told me the following when I became *Sarkaryavah*. He said, "All people are basically nice. One should deal with every person by believing in his goodness. Anger, jealousy, etc. are offshoots of his past experiences, which affect his behaviour. Primarily, every person is nice and everyone is reliable. We should accept this when dealing with people."

At least two to three times he told me that anger never proved helpful. He even said that during his work in the Sangh, he became angry twice or thrice and all the times he suffered some loss; gained nothing. I feel that to exercise control over one's anger and behaviour, one has to keep a well-balanced mind and this he had achieved.

The capacity to treat all persons in the same manner and consider all people good and reliable helped him take many people along with him. He never mentioned his difficulties; he remained engrossed in Sangh activities.

A few days ago, I went to attend a meeting of the Vishwa Hindu Parishad. During an informal discussion, Acharya Dharmendraji told me that once when Rajju Bhaiya was in Mumbai, he too happened to be there. When Acharya Dharmendraji went to meet Rajju Bhaiya, the latter was having his breakfast. The meal was so spicy that only one look at his face conveyed everything to Dharmendraji, who could not help remarking, "Rajju Bhaiya, why are you swallowing this poison? What pleasure are you deriving from eating so much of chilies in the food?"

Then Rajju Bhaiya opened his mouth to reveal his tongue. There were boils on his tongue. Acharya Dharmendra suggested him to ask for something else, like porridge for instance.

But Rajju Bhaiya replied, "No, a very old Swayamsevak has brought this meal for me with great love; that's why I am eating it." This shows that Rajju Bhaiya was more concerned about the Swayamsevak than for his own discomfort.

Once Rajju Bhaiya came to Nagpur on a short tour. He was *Sarkaryavah* at that time and I was a *Pracharak* in Nagpur. Normally, when any Adhikari comes to Nagpur, his itinerary is chalked out for a continuous stay of two to three days. Hence, about five to six programmes were arranged for him to attend daily. That day, after attending his morning schedule, he reached the *Sangh Karyalaya* (RSS Office). I was accompanying him to escort him to his room when my hand inadvertently touched his hand. I felt as though I had touched the burning amber. I immediately took hold of his hand and felt his body burning with fever. I said, "You have temperature." He replied, "Don't worry; it has been continuing since the past two-three days."

I said, "No, No, the schedule..."

He cut me short, "No, don't cancel the programme. I have to talk while sitting; it would be no strain on the body. I am able to walk and as I am eating food too, I can surely talk." He attended all the programmes.

He would keep himself in the background and the ideal in the forefront. This was the second prime quality of his personality. In the modern times, I think these two qualities are very essential for every Swayamsevak.

Once in a semi-conscious state, Rajju Bhaiya had said,

"The Sangh work is increasing; need is for increasing the tempo. Work can be expedited only when each Swayamsevak gives supremacy to Sangh work. Let him be a student, a householder or an ascetic, every Swayamsevak has to accept that Sangh work comes first, while the rest is secondary. When such a situation is reached, the momentum of Sangh work will get a fillip." Rajju Bhaiya set the example with his own life: Sangh work first; I come second.

Secondly, we all should forever remember Rajju Bhaiya's *moolmantra* (watch-word): All people are primarily good, all are reliable to work for bringing unity in the society.

Only the Sangh Swayamsevaks have the capacity to take the entire society along with them. I think, to fulfil the objective of the next phase of Sangh work, the two main qualities that every Swayamsevak should have are which Rajju Bhaiya conveyed through his personal life."

□

13

K.S. Sudarshan: The Fifth RSS Chief

The Fifth RSS Chief – Kuppahalli Sitaramayya Sudarshan – hailed from Mandya District in Karnataka. He served as RSS *Sarasanghchalak*, the Chief of the Organisation from 2000 to 2009 when he stepped down due to health and handed over the charge of the organisation to Mohanrao Bhagwat, the sixth and the present RSS Chief.

The fifth RSS Chief was known for his sharp intellect, wisdom and deep knowledge of wide range of subjects ranging from

Hinduism to foreign affairs. He had the ability to assimilate the global and Indian trends at macro level and paint the big picture in a theoretical framework for even common Swayamsevaks.

His discourses were popular among even those who were not Swayamsevaks. Born on June 18, 1931 in Raipur (it was part of Madhya Pradesh at that time), Sudarshan joined the RSS *Shakha* at the age of nine.

He was a sharp student and finished his Bachelor of Engineering in Telecommunications (honours) from Sagar University. In 1954, he decided to become a fulltime worker of the RSS and became a *Pracharak.*

As a *Pracharak,* his first stint was in Raigarh district. At a fairly young age of 33, he became *Prant* (Province) *Pracharak,* of *Madhya Bharat* (Central India region) in 1964.

In 1969, when he was 38, he received the national responsibility as, *Akhil Bharatiya Sharirik Pramukh* (All India in-charge of physical activities). He was one of handpicked RSS cadre by the then *Sarasanghchalak* M.S. Golwalkar.

This was followed by a stint in the North-East (1977) and then two years later he took over as the Akhil Bharatiya Bouddhik Pramukh (All India in-charge of intellectual cell).

In 1990, he was appointed *Sah-Sarkaryavah* (Joint General Secretary) of the organisation. He has the rare distinction of having held both posts of Sharirik (physical exercises) and Bauddhik (intellectual) Pramukh (Chief) on different occasions. In 2000, he became *Sarsanghchalak* of RSS.

A strong votary of Swadeshi, he was one of the key ideologues of RSS. He breathed his last on September 15, 2012 at Raipur in Chhattisgarh.

Several national leaders expressed their condolences. Prime Minister Narendra Modi, who was the Chief Minister of Gujarat at the time of demise of Sudarshan, said about him, "He was blessed with a sharp mind, humorous nature and always known for his simple and disciplined life."

Remembering Sudarshan, a senior former RSS functionary, wrote for Rediff.com, "In RSS *Karyalayas*

(office-cum-residence), he made it an unwritten rule followed by all to only fill as much water in the glass as one is sure to drink. 'Don't waste water, don't fill up the glass only to throw it into the wash-basin. Water is sacred and scarce,' he would urge."

He tried to persuade everyone he met to stop ostentatious marriages. Don't go in for such celebrations, it's a mockery of India's poor millions and a blot on Hindu society. And so was his mission to fight female foeticide. We worship Lakshmi, Durga and Saraswati as stone idols but kill them in the womb, he said in a speech.

"Very often, whenever he happened to be in Delhi, he would come to the offices of *Panchjanya* and *Organiser* and discuss several contemporary issues with the editors. His knowledge of global affairs and their likely impact on India was awesome. His friends' circle included diplomats, scientists, Vedic scholars, environmentalists and economists espousing the cause of Swadeshi."

"He was fond of Atal Bihari Vajpayee's poems and would recite many of them verbatim at several meetings. So, when a daily newspaper published his interview that created awkwardness between him and Vajpayee ji, he felt sad about it. And it goes to the credit of both leaders' maturity that the bad blood was removed and relations normalised," added this former RSS functionary.

Sudarshan is known to have studied Islam very closely. He was a respected figure in Islamic world also, busting the misconception yet again about the RSS and the Muslims.

A report in Dailybhaskar.com published a few days after Sudarshan's demise sums this up: "Islamic organisation Jamaat-e-Islami Hind (JIH) has surprisingly praised former RSS Chief K. Sudarshan and deeply mourned his death."

In an article published in the September 22 issue of JIH bi-weekly mouthpiece *Dawat*, "Why did they feel sad at his death?", Chief Editor Rahmani wrote, "It is not known how sad the Sangh Parivar felt at the demise of K.S. Sudarshan." But, the "Muslims, who on August 20 would have heard or read the news from Bhopal", must have been sad.

Earlier, in *Dawat's* September 1 issue, Rahmani had called Sudarshan one of the, "oldest and most important leaders" of the RSS and a well-educated person.

According to a *Times of India* report, Dawat's chief editor Parwaaz Rahmani recounted how Sudarshan wanted to visit Bhopal's Tajul Masjid on August 20 "to say the *Eid* prayer or to offer *Eid* greetings"...

After the *Eid namaz*, former MP Chief Minister, Babulal Gaur took him to the house of a Muslim acquaintance where Sudarshan offered Eid greetings, enjoyed *sewaiyan* (a sweet dish) and was pleased, Rahmani wrote.

Sudarshan's remarks on the need for having 'Swadeshi' Church evoked a huge debate in 2001. It all started when he spoke at a book release function. The RSS weekly 'Orgainser' carried a dated report (April 29, 2001) of this function. The report titled "Set up federation of Swadeshi churches in India" provided an insight into the thought process of the fifth RSS chief.

"Rashtriya Swayamsevak Sangh (RSS) *Sarsanghchalak* Shri K.S. Sudarshan called for forming a federation of Indian Christians who subscribed to the idea of a Swadeshi Church. This, according to him, would be the first step towards the creation of the National Church in India, which would be free from the foreign controls of all kinds."

□

14

Mohan Bhagwat: The Sixth RSS Chief

Dr. Mohan Madhukar Rao Bhagwat, commonly known as Mohan Bhagwat, was born on September 11, 1950 at Chandrapur in Maharashtra. His father, Madhukar Rao Bhagwat, was also a dedicated Swayamsevak, who also worked as a *Pracharak*. Mohan is the eldest son of his parents and has two younger brothers and a sister.

He finished his schooling from 'Lokmanya Tilak Vidyalaya'. He also studied at Janta College in

Chandrapur. Later, he graduated in Veterinary Sciences and Animal Husbandry from 'Punjabrao Agriculture University, at Akola in Maharashtra.

Dr. Bhagwat left his post-graduate studies in-between to become a *Pracharak* of the RSS towards the end of 1975. He went underground after Emergency was imposed in 1975 and worked extensively to oppose the draconian measures initiated by the then Congress government led by the then Prime Minister Indira Gandhi.

From 1991 to 1999, he was 'Akhil Bharatiya Sharirik Pramukh', (national in-charge of physical training). Later, he was given to shoulder the responsibility of full-time RSS workers, i.e. *Pracharak* as 'Akhil Bharatiya *Pracharak* Pramukh', (in-charge of RSS volunteers working full-time for India).

In the year 2000, he was appointed as *Sarkaryavah*, (General Secretary). On March 21, 2009, he was appointed as the *Sarsanghchalak*. He is one of the youngest RSS Chiefs in its history and highly respected for his organisational skills and decisiveness. The RSS has been expanding its footprint with a new vigour under his leadership.

To get an insight about the perspective with which the Sixth RSS Chief looks at various issues, one needs to go through his annual speech at Nagpur, delivered on the occasion of 'Vijaya Dashmi' in the year 2014. One must remember here that 2014 witnessed a historical political victory for the Bharatiya Janta Party led by an RSS Swayamsevak, who became Prime Minister of the country. In this context, when one reads the speech, there is clear realisation that, undeterred by the trappings of the political power, RSS is evolving its vision at its own pace and on its own terms.

□

THE CONSTITUTION OF THE RASHTRIYA SWAYAMSEVAK SANGH

(The Constitution of
The Rashtriya Swayamsevak Sangh
as adopted on 1st August 1949 and
amended upto 12th March 2008)

***

(Translated from the original in Hindi)
(as adopted on 1st August, 1949 and
amended upto 1st July, 1972)

PREAMBLE

WHEREAS in the disintegrated condition of the country, it was considered necessary to have an organisation,

(a) to eradicate the fissiparous tendencies arising from diversities of sect, faith, caste and creed and from political, economic, linguistic and provincial differences, amongst Hindus;

(b) to make them realise the greatness of their past;

(c) to inculcate in them a spirit of service, sacrifice and selfless devotion to the Society;

(d) to build up an organised and well-disciplined corporate life; and

(e) to bring about an all-round regeneration of the Hindu Samaj on the basis of its Dharma and its Sanskriti;

AND WHEREAS the organisation known as 'RASHTRIYA SWAYAMSEVAK SANGH' was started on the Vijaya Dashami day in the year 1982 Vikram Samvat

(1925 A.D.) by the late Dr. Keshav Baliram Hedgewar;

AND WHEREAS Shri Madhav Sadashiv Golwalkar was nominated by the said Dr. Hedgewar to succeed him in the year 1997 Vikram Samvat (1940 A.D.);

AND WHEREAS the Sangh had till now no written Constitution;

AND WHEREAS in the present changed conditions, it is deemed desirable to reduce to writing the Constitution as also the Aims and Objects of the Sangh and its Methods of Work,

THE RASHTRIYA SWAYAMSEVAK SANGH hereby adopts the following Constitution:

ARTICLE- 1

NAME

The name of the Organisation is 'RASHTRIYA SWAYAMSEVAK SANGH.'

ARTICLE- 2

HEAD QUARTERS

The Head quarters of the Akhil Bharatiya Karyakari Mandal are at NAGPUR.

ARTICLE- 3

AIMS AND OBJECTS

The Aims and Objects of the Sangh are to weld together the various diverse groups within the Hindu Samaj and to revitalise and rejuvenate the same on the basis of its Dharma and Sanskriti, that it may achieve an all-sided development of Bharatvarsha.

ARTICLE -4

POLICY

(a) The Sangh believes in the orderly evolution of

society and adheres to peaceful and legitimate means for the realisation of its ideals.

(b) In consonance with the cultural heritage of the Hindu Samaj, the Sangh has abiding faith in the fundamental principle of respect towards all faiths.

(c) The Sangh is aloof from politics and is devoted to social and cultural fields only. However, the Swayamsevaks are free, as individuals, to join any party, institution, or front, political or otherwise, except such parties, institutions, or fronts which subscribe to or believe in extra-national loyalties, or resort to violent and/or secret activities to achieve their ends, or which promote or attempt to promote, or have the object of promoting any feeling of enmity or hatred towards any other community or creed or religious denomination. Persons owing allegiance to the above-mentioned undesirable elements and methods of working shall have no place in the Sangh.

ARTICLE -5

DHWAJ

While recognising the duty of every citizen to be loyal to and to respect the State Flag, the Sangh has as its flag, the 'BHAGWA-DHWAJ'—the age-old symbol of Hindu Sanskriti which the Sangh regards as its 'GURU'.

ARTICLE -6

SWAYAMSEVAK

1 (a) Any male Hindu of 18 years or above, who subscribes to the Aims and Objects of the Sangh and conforms generally to its discipline and

associates himself with the activities of the Shakha will be considered as a Swayamsevak.

(b) A Swayamsevak shall be deemed to be an Active Swayamsevak if he pledges to devote himself for the furtherance of the Aims and Objects of the Sangh, and attends a Shakha regularly or performs any work duly assigned to him.

(c) A Swayamsevak shall cease to be a Swayamsevak if he resigns or is removed for any act prejudicial to the interests of the Shakha or the Sangh.

2. **Bal Swayamsevak**—Any male Hindu below the age of 18 may be admitted and allowed to participate in the Shakha programmes as a Bal Swayamsevak.

ARTICLE -7

SHAKHA

(a) Swayamsevaks desirous of propagating the Aims and Objects of the Sangh coming together in the form of a regular assemblage will form a Centre. Each Centre shall be a self-contained unit receiving its finances and making its own financial disbursements and is herein referred to as a 'SHAKHA'.

(b) Each such Shakha shall constitute the primary unit of the Sangh, which shall be an autonomous body in respect of its administration and finances.

(c) The Shakha shall function under the directions of its Karyakari Mandal.

ARTICLE- 8

PROGRAMMES

For the fulfilment of the Aims and Objects as set out herein earlier, the Shakhas may undertake any or all of the following programmes:

'Arranging frequent discussions and lectures for imparting intellectual and moral education to Swayamsevaks and others and inculcating in them love for the Nation and the ideals of Hindu Dharma and Sanskriti.

'Establishing and running of Libraries and Reading Rooms for the benefit of the general public.

'Carrying on of activities or undertaking programmes for the welfare and benefit of the general public, such as extending medical care, propagation of literacy and improvement of living conditions of the poorer sections of the society; and flood and famine relief, study circles and free exhibition of educative films and advancement of other objects of general public utility, but not involving carrying on of activity for profit.

'Imparting physical education by means of exercises and games with a view to improving the physical and mental faculties of Swayamsevaks and others for the co-ordinated and disciplined development of the Society.

'Arranging periodical classes for Swayamsevaks to be trained as Instructors and Workers.

'Celebrating festivals of cultural importance with a view to providing opportunity for Swayamsevaks and others to imbibe the sublime cultural values of character, service and sacrifice to rededicate themselves to the cause of society.

'Adopting suitable means and establishing institutions to propagate the ideals and activities of the Sangh and to educate the people.

'Generally, the Shakhas may do all such things as are considered necessary and are conducive, directly or indirectly, to promoting and achieving any of the objects of the Sangh.'

ARTICLE- 9

FINANCES

Any voluntary offering made with devotion before the BHAGWA-DHWAJ shall exclusively constitute the finances of the Shakha and shall belong to and be solely managed and disbursed by the Shakha for the promotion of the Aims and Objects of the Sangh and general advancement of Sangh work to be done by the Shakha according to the rules framed by it for that purpose.

ARTICLE -10

ELECTIONS

(a) Elections shall be held after every three years.

(b) The date, method and venue of election shall be determined by the concerned K.M. in consultation with the A.B.K.M.

ARTICLE -11

QUALIFICATION FOR VOTERS AND CANDIDATES FOR ELECTIONS AND APPOINTEES

(a) VOTERS

Every Active Swayamsevak of at least one-year

standing immediately prior to the date of preparation of the Electoral lists in the election shall be entitled to vote in the election.

(b) CANDIDATES FOR ELECTIONS AND APPOINTEES

(1) A Swayamsevak, who is an office-bearer of a political party, shall not be eligible as a candidate for election or as an appointee to any post so long as he is such an office-bearer.

(2) A candidate for election, or an appointee to any Akhil Bharatiya post, shall be an Active Swayamsevak of at least six years' continuous standing.

(3) A candidate or appointee for Sanghachalakship shall be an Active Swayamsevak of at least one-year standing.

ARTICLE -12

SARSANGHCHALAK

The late Dr. Keshav Baliram Hedgewar, the founder of the Sangh, was the Adya (First) Sarsanghchalak. He, in consultation with the then K.K.M., nominated Shri Madhav Sadashiv Golwalkar, who is the Sarsanghchalak since then. The Sarsanghchalak will nominate his successor as and when the necessity arises, with the consent of the then A.B.K.M.

The Sarsanghchalak is the Guide and Philosopher of the Rashtriya Swayamsevak Sangh. He may attend, summon or address any assembly of the Swayamsevaks, A.B.P.S. and Karyakari Mandals severally or jointly.

ARTICLE -13

SARKARYAVAHA

(a) The elected members of the Akhil Bharatiya Pratinidhi Sabha (vide Article 15a) shall elect the Sarkaryavaha.

(b) The Sarkaryavaha shall act in consultation with the Sarsanghchalak.

(c) In case of death, incapacity, or resignation of the Sarkaryavaha, the A.B.K.M. may appoint a person to discharge his duties until such time as his successor is elected.

ARTICLE -14

AKHIL BHARATIYA KARYAKARI MANDAL

(a) The Sarkaryavaha shall form the Akhil Bharatiya Karyakari Mandal of which he shall be the Chairman with the following office-bearers duly appointed by him:

i. One or more Sah-Sarkaryavahas.

ii. Akhil Bharatiya Sharirik Shikshan Pramukh. (In-charge of guidance in physical education.)

iii. Akhil Bharatiya Bouddhik Shikshan Pramukh. (In-charge of guidance in intellectual and moral instruction.)

iv. Akhil Bharatiya Prachar Pramukh (In-charge of propagation of Sangh work and guidance to Pracharaks).

v. Akhil Bharatiya Vyavastha Pramukh. (In-charge of general management), and not less than five members chosen from among the Prantiya Karyakari Mandals.

(b) The following will be the functions of the A.B.K.M. –

i. The A.B.K.M is the co-ordinating body of all of the Shakhas in the country to carry out the policies and programmes laid down by the A.B.P.S.

ii. The A.B.K.M. will frame rules and bye-laws in consonance with the Constitution for the purpose of regulating its own affairs and for the general functioning of the Sangh.

ARTICLE- 15

AKHIL BHARATIYA PRATINIDHI SABHA

(a) The delegates elected in accordance with Article 16 (a) and (i) and (ii) in a Prant shall elect from amongst themselves one-tenth of their number as representatives of the Shakhas on the Akhil Bharatiya Pratinidhi Sabha.

(b) The A.B.P.S-shall consist of :

i. Representatives of the Shakhas as elected in 15(a) above,

ii. Sanghachalak and Pracharaks of Vibhags and Prants.

iii. Members of the A.B.K.M.

(c) The Sarkaryavaha shall be the chairman of the A.B.P.S.

(d) The A.B.P.S shall meet at least once a year.

(e) The A.B.P.S shall review the work and lay down policy and programmes of the Sangh.

ARTICLE- 16

DELEGATES AND SANGHACHALAKS

(a) i. Fifty or more Swayamsevaks entitled to vote in Shakha will elect from among themselves one for every fifty such Swayamsevaks as delegates of the Shakha.

ii. Such of the Shakhas as are having less than fifty Swayamsevaks entitled to vote will come together to elect delegates.

(b) The delegates, as elected above, in a Jilla, in a Vibhag and in a Prant will elect the Jilla Sanghachalak, the Vibhag Sanghachalak and the Prant Sanghachalak, respectively.

(c) The Jilla Sanghachalak, in consultation with the Prant Sanghachalak and Prant Pracharak will nominate Sanghachalak' for the various Shakhas and groups of Shakhas within the Jilla.

(d) In case a suitable person is not available for the office of Sanghachalak, the Jilla Sanghachalak will appoint a Karyavaha.

(e) In case of death, incapacity or resignation of Prant, Vibhag or Jilla Sanghachalak, the K.M. of the larger area may appoint a person to discharge the duties of the respective Sanghachalak until such time as his successor is elected.

ARTICLE -17

PRACHARAKS

(a) i. Pracharaks shall be fulltime workers selected from amongst those devoted workers of high integrity, whose mission is to serve the society through the Sangh and who, of their own free will, dedicate themselves to the Cause,

ii. They will receive no remuneration. However, their expenses will be met by the Shakhas.

(b) Appointment of Pracharaks :

i. The Sarkaryavaha will appoint Prant Pracharaks on the advice of the Akhil Bharatiya Prachar Pramukh and in consultation with the Prant Sanghachalak concerned.

ii. The Prant Sanghachalak on the advice of Prant Pracharak will appoint Pracharaks for different areas in the Prant for the assistance and co-ordination of the Shakhas in their respective areas.

ARTICLE -18

KARYAKARI MANDALS

(a) Sanghachalak of a Prant, Vibhag or Jilla elected in accordance with 16(b), or any group of Shakhas within the Jilla appointed in accordance with 16(c), will form a Karyakari Mandal of the respective area, of which he shall be the Chairman, consisting of the following office bearers duly appointed by him :

i. Karyavaha
ii. Pracharak (appointed under Article 17(b)(ii)
iii. Sharirik Shikshan Pramukh
iv. Bouddhik Shikshan Pramukh
v. Vyavastha Pramukh

(b) The Sanghachalak of a Shakha appointed in accordance with 16(c) will form a Karyakari Mandal, of which he shall be the Chairman, consisting of the following office-bearers duly appointed by him :

i. Karyavaha
ii. Sharirik Shikshan Pramukh
iii. Bouddhik Shikshan Pramukh

iv. Prachar Pramukh

v. Vyavastha Pramukh

vi) Nidhi Pramukh

NOTE : In case suitable person/s is/are not available for appointment to any one or more of the above posts, the same may remain vacant until suitable person/s is/are available.

(c) Each Karyakari Mandal shall also have, in addition, not less than three members chosen from amongst the other Karyakari Mandals within the area, if any.

(d) K.M.s, will be executive bodies in their respective areas, guided by the K.M. of the immediate larger area for implementing the policy and carrying out the programme laid down by the A.B.P.S.

(e) The K.M. of a Shakha will have the power to take disciplinary action against any individual Swayamsevak for breach of discipline or behaviour prejudicial to the interests of the Shakha or the Sangh. Such an action will be subject to confirmation by the Karyakari Mandal of the immediate larger area.

ARTICLE -19

QUORUM

Onehalf of the total strength shall form the QUORUM for the meetings of the various Karyakari Mandals, and onefifth lot in A.B.P.S.

ARTICLE -20

UNDEVELOPED PRANTS

In case of prants in which the work has not yet

developed to an appreciable level, the A.B.K.M. may provide representation to them on the A.B.P.S. in a manner it deems fit.

ARTICLE -21

INTERPRETATION AND AMENDMENTS TO CONSTITUTION

(a) The interpretation of the Constitution and its Articles by the A.B.K.M shall be final.

(b) An amendment to the Constitution not inconsistent with the Aims and Objects of the Sangh can be proposed at a convention specially convened for that purpose by the A.B.K.M. on its own, or to the A.B.K.M. by any P.K.M., or by any other Karyakari Mandal with the recommendation of the respective P.K.M., or by any twenty-five members of the A.B.P.S. The A.B.K.M. after due consideration will, put the proposal of such an amendment before the P.K.M.s, and the amendment will be deemed carried if two-thirds of the P.K.M.s agree by simple majority.

(c) The decision of the P.K.M.s regarding such amendments may be brought for reconsideration before the A.B.P.S. on a requisition by any twenty-five members of that Sabha. The decision of the A.B.P.S. in this behalf, taken by a two-thirds majority, shall be final.

(Source: Sanjeev Kelkar, *Lost Years of the RSS, 2011 edition)*

□

Appendix-2

Rashtriya Swayamsevak Sangh: Timeline

1925 – Doctor Kesava Rao Baliram Hedgewar (Doctorji), the founder of Sangh, announced on Vijayadasami day, September 27, that "we are inaugurating the sangh today. All of us must train ourselves physically, intellectually and in every way so as to be capable of achieving our cherished goal."

1926 – The name 'Rashtriya Swayamsevak Sangh' was selected for Sangh on April 17. Daily meetings. Nitya Shakhas were started at Mohitewada ground in Nagpur on 28th May.

1928 – First Guru Dakshina Utsavam held with a total contribution – samarpana – of ₹ 84. First winter camp was organised.

1929 – In a meeting on 9, 10 Nov. held at Doke Math, Nagpur, Doctor Hedgewar was designated as the Chief [Sarsangh chalak], Balaji Huddar as General Secretary [sarkaryavaha] and Marthanda Rao Jog as Chief Trainer [sarsenapathi].

1931 – RSS started its daily shakha in Varanasi, Bhayyaji Dhani introduced MS Golwalkar to shakha in Benares.

1932 – Central Province Government issued orders on December 15 prohibiting government employees from participating in RSS.

1935 – The order prohibiting Government employees from participating in RSS was defeated in the legislative assembly. Mahatma Gandhiji Visited the RSS camp in Vardha. MS Golwalkar also known as 'Guruji' was designated as 'Karyavaha' of Nagpur Shakha.

1936 - Rashtra Sevika Samiti was founded on Vijayadahmi, 25 Oct. RSS started work in Punjab.

1937 - RSS started work in Uttar Pradesh. Batch of 10 Swayamseveks was sent for the purpose.

1939 - M.S. Golwalkar designated as national General Secretary (Sarkaryavaha).

1940 - Subhas Chandra Bose visited Doctor Hedgewar on his deathbed on June 20. Dr. Hedgewar passed away on 21 June. Golwalkar becomes the new RSS chief.

1947 - In Kenya, RSS swayamsevaks started 'Bharatiya Swayamsevak Sangh'. Two weeklies-Organizer (English) and Panchajanya (Hindi) launched.

1948 - Mahatma Gandhi killed, RSS banned, more than 17000 swayamsevaks including Golwalkar arrested.

1949 - Ban on RSS lifted. The RSS drafted its Constitution. The RSS launched 'Akhil Bharatiya Vidyardhi Parishad (ABVP)' to work among college students.

1950 - First meeting of Akhil Bharatiya Pratinidhi Sabha. Bhaiyyaji Dani elected Sarkaryavah [general secretary].

1952 - Cow Protection Movement – Goraksha Andolan – was launched demanding prohibition of cow slaughter in the country. Swayamsevaks collected 1,75,39,813 signatures covering every part of the country from 85,000 cities and villages. All these signatures were presented to the President of Bharat, Dr. Rajendra Prasad, on 8 December. Vanvasi Kalayan Asharam Started. Bharatiya Jansangh was formed by Dr. Shyama Prasad Mukherjee and many Swayamsevaks joined it.

1953 - Sudden demise of Dr. Syama Prasada Mukherjee in Kashmir on 23 June.

1954 - RSS Swayamsevaks liberated Dadra and Nagar Haveli from Portugese control on August 2 and handed over the region to Central Government.

1955 - Bharatiya Mazdoor Sangh was founded. RSS Swayamsevaks lead the all-party struggle for the liberation of Goa from the control of Portugese.

1956 - Eknath Ranade was elected Sarkaryavah.

1962 - Bhaiyyaji Dani was elected Sarkaryavah. China attacked India, RSS swayamsevaks mobilised support for Indian government and security forces.

1963 - RSS was invited to participate in the Republic Day Parade on January 26 in Delhi. Around 3000 swayamsevaks with full uniform and band participated in this parade.

1965 - Madhukar Dattatreya Deoras (Balasahebji) was elected as General Secretary(Sarkaryavaha). Pakistan attacked India, RSS swayamsevaks led blood donation efforts and contributed to war efforts. Golwalkar participated in All Party Conference convened by the then Prime Minister Lal Bahadur Shastri.

1973 - The second RSS Chief MS Golwalkar passed away on June 5. Balasaheb Deoras was designated as third Sarsangh Chalak on June 6.

Mahavrao Muley was elected as Sarkaryavah.

1975 - Emergency imposed on June 25, RSS banned for the second time on July 4. Balasaheb and several other RSS leaders arrested. RSS led from front the movement against emergency.

1977 - Ban on RSS lifted on March 22. Jayprakash Narayan addressed the RSS meeting in Patna on November 3. Prof. Rajendra Singh designated as Saha Sarkaryavaha – Joint General Secretary.

1978 - Madhava Rao Moole, Sarkayavaha, passed away on September 30. Prof. Rajendra Singh was elected as Sarkayavaha.

1980 - RSS launched mass public contact programme – Jana samparka abhiyan – covering 95000 villages and 1 crore families.

1981 - Sanskar Bharti founded. RSS led nationwide campaign against conversions after 800 Hindus at Meenakshipuram in Kerala converted to Islam.

1985 - RSS completed 60 years. Nation-wide awareness programmes were conducted.

1986 - Rashtriya Sikh Sangat was founded.

1987 - HV Seshadri was elected Sarkaryavah.

1989 - On June 25, the terrorist attacked an RSS Shakha in Moga, Punjab killing 18 Swayamsevaks and 6 others. Atleast 28 persons were injured.

1992 - Bhau Rao Desoras passed away on May 14. Yadavrao Joshi passed away on August 20. Babri structure on Ram Janmabhoomi was removed by karsevaks on December 6. The central government banned Sangh for the third time on December 10.

1993 - Bahri Tribunal found the ban on Sangh unjustified and the ban was lifted on June 4. Akhil

Bharatiya Poorva Sainik Seva Parishad was founded.

1994 - Prof. Rajendra Singh (Rajju Bhaiya) was designated as 4th Sarsangh Chalak of RSS on March 11.

- Akhil Bharatiya Seva Vibhag Started. Laghu Udyog Bharati was founded.

1996 - Balasheb Deoras passed away on June 17.

1999 - Four full time workers (Pracharaks) - Dinendranath Day, Shayamalkanti Sen, Shubhankar Chakravarti and Sudhayamay Datta - were abducted in Tripura by NLFT militants on August 6 demanding a ransom of ₹ 2 crores. Later all the four pracharaks were killed.

2000 - K.S. Sudershan nominated as RSS chief, Mohan Bhagwat elected as General Secretary.

2003 - Prof. Rajendra Singh and senior RSS Pracharaks Moropant Pingley and Chamanlal passed away.

2004 - Dattopant Thengadi, stalwart of Labour and Swadeshi movement and a key ideologue, passed away.

2005 - H.V. Seshadri Passed away.

2009 - Mohan Bhagwat becomes the new RSS chief.

2012 - K.S. Sudarshan passed away.

□□□